NATIVE STORIERS

Native Storiers

A Series of American Narratives

SERIES EDITORS

Gerald Vizenor

Diane Glancy

NATIVE STORIERS

FIVE SELECTIONS

EDITED AND WITH
AN INTRODUCTION
BY GERALD VIZENOR

UNIVERSITY OF NEBRASKA PRESS
LINCOLN AND LONDON

Selections from *Bleed into Me: A Book of Stories* by Stephen Graham Jones are reprinted by permission of the University of Nebraska Press. © 2005 by Stephen Graham Jones.

Selections from *Mending Skins* by Eric Gansworth are reprinted by permission of the University of Nebraska Press. © 2005 by Eric Gansworth.

Selections from *Elsie's Business* by Frances Washburn are reprinted by permission of the author. © 2006 by Frances Washburn.

Selections from *Hiroshima Bugi: Atomu 57* by Gerald Vizenor are reprinted by permission of the University of Nebraska Press. © 2003 by Gerald Vizenor.

Selections from *Designs of the Night Sky* by Diane Glancy are reprinted by permission of the University of Nebraska Press. © 2002 by Diane Glancy.

Manufactured in the
United States of America
∞

Library of Congress
Cataloging-in-Publication Data
Native storiers : five selections / edited and with an introduction by Gerald Vizenor.
p. cm. — (Native storiers)
ISBN 978-0-8032-1717-1
(pbk. : alk. paper)
1. American fiction—Indian authors.
2. American fiction—20th century.
3. Indians of North America—Fiction.
I. Vizenor, Gerald Robert, 1934–
PS508.I5N387 2009
813'.6080897—dc22
2008025875

Set in Iowan Old Style and Lithos
by Kim Essman.
Designed by R. W. Boeche.

CONTENTS

Introduction 1

Bleed into Me
Stephen Graham Jones 9

Mending Skins
Eric Gansworth 45

Elsie's Business
Frances Washburn 71

Hiroshima Bugi: Atomu 57
Gerald Vizenor 115

Designs of the Night Sky
Diane Glancy 165

Contributors 197

INTRODUCTION

GERALD VIZENOR

"The books have voices. I hear them in the library," writes Diane Glancy in *Designs of the Night Sky*. "I know the voices are from the books. Yet I know the old stories do not like books. Do not like the written words. Do not like libraries. The old stories carry all the voices of those who have told them. When a story is spoken, all those voices are in the voice of the narrator. But writing the words of a story kills the voices that gather in the sound of the storytelling. The story is singular then. Only one voice travels in the written words. One voice is not enough to tell a story. Yet I can hear a voice telling its story in the archives of the university library. I hear the books. Not with my ears, but in my imagination. Maybe the voices camp in the library because the written words hold them there. Maybe they are captives with no place else to go."

Designs of the Night Sky is the first of five books published in Native Storiers: A Series of American Narratives by the University of Nebraska Press. The selections in this anthology are from *Bleed into Me* by Stephen Graham Jones, *Mending Skins* by Eric Gansworth, *Elsie's Business* by Frances Washburn, *Hiroshima Bugi: Atomu 57* by Gerald Vizenor, and *Designs of the Night Sky*.

The Native Storiers series considers innovative, emergent novels and avant-garde narratives created by Native American Indians. The authors of these original narratives create a style that portrays unusual and diverse characters, experiences, and points of view in stories that arise from inseparable, actuated traditions past and present. The series editors invite a wide range of literary styles of fiction that register, construct, or depict a perception and ethos of survivance. The series considers novellas; short, interrelated stories; and other narratives that may tease modes, styles, voices, points of view, identities, ideologies, and, by literary contravention, trickster stories that would bemuse cultural boundaries and dominance. The narratives and stories considered for publication in this new series create an innovative sense of survivance over the conventional themes of tragic victimry.

"Columbus landed in the second grade for me, and my teacher made me swallow the names of the boats one by one until in the bathtub of my summer vacation I opened my mouth and they came back out—Niña, Pinta, Santa Maria," writes Stephen Graham Jones in *Bleed into Me*. The boats "bobbed on the surface of the water like toys. I clapped my hand over my mouth once, Indian style, then looked up, for my mother, so she could pull the plug, stop all this, but when I opened my mouth again it was just blood and blood and blood."

The innovative narratives in this series bear the traces of oral storiers and, at the same time, initiate a new aesthetic convergence of literary art. Clearly there are many cultural distinctions, ambiguities, exceptions, and inconsistencies, but the literary practices, pleasures, and original flight of these storiers are more significant than the mere simulations of commercial romance and victimry.

Native narratives that easily reach a wide audience may portray the generic simulations of tragic victimry, that familiar sentiment in literature. Tragedy is a serious occidental practice, an imitation of action that may represent the demise of character or fortune in literature and popular culture. Native storiers create action in scenes and characters by natural reason, visionary motion, transformations of nature, and by an active sense of presence and survivance. Many readers are more accustomed to the tropes of realism, character motivation more than transformation, and the simulations of tragic victimry.

The selections in this volume, all from the Native Storiers series, demonstrate a distinctive literary aesthetic. Native storiers, the ancestors of modern writers, created a sense of presence by natural reason, sound, motion, and traces of seasons; by imagic, totemic associations of birds and animals; by transmutations; and by evasive, unrehearsed trickster stories. The ethos of presence, natural reason, survivance, spirited transmotion, tricky conversions of reality, and a visionary motion of continental liberty, is the unmistakable cue and trace of a new aesthetic in the literature of Native American Indians.

"Forgetting. That's what this is really about: trying to sort out those times in your experience with someone that you'd just as soon not have to carry around with you for the rest of your life. They tell you it's about remembering, when they try to sell your family the inspiration cards with your entry and exit dates and some moving verse," writes Eric Gansworth in *Mending Skins*.

These suspension straps lower me into the hole then slide out from under me, and the last ritual begins. They want to pretend they're helping to bury me, my last mortal remains, but what they really drop down into this deep hole are memories, unwanted, muddy thickly clotted memories, laced with roots and worms and beetles, the occasional termite.

My father is first. I recognize his hand immediately. He lets the dirt fall in hard clumps, hitting the top of my urn. I wonder if he's using two hands to pick up a large enough chunk. He's looking to make a dent, leave a mark, anything. . . .

My mother is second and even a little unsteady in the way she tosses the dirt in. She sprinkles it like she would powdered sugar on top of fry bread on occasion. She doesn't want to give up that many memories, but I know the ones she's dusting me with. They are those last few weekends I come home on leave, saving all my pay so I can get back here, and she grows more and more busy every time I return. That last time she asks me not to come back, that it's too hard to see me leave, and I can see she'll be relieved when I head out for Vietnam for good, so she can begin the forgetting process in earnest. She's been rehearsing for this minute going on five years.

Native ancestral storiers hunted their words by memory, sound, shadow, chance, ecstatic conversions, and by the uncertainties of nature, seasons, constant creations. Native literary artists create the tropes of oral stories in the silence of narratives and in the imagic scenes of eternal motion, totemic transmutation, pronoun waves, gender obversion, animal presence, protean voices, and in a sense of survivance. These aesthetic practices alight in the innovative stories and narratives of many Native American Indians.

"The ceremony is ended. The people are lining up for the giveaway. Oscar pushes you into line, and you move forward shuffling in the snow. The woman ahead of you says to her companion something about that red blanket on the end and she hopes it's still there when it's her turn. The line moves forward, pauses, moves forward, and the pile dwindles some and it's your turn, but you stand there and wonder what on earth you would do with any of this stuff. You could always use the groceries, but it feels silly to carry it back on the bus," writes Frances Washburn in *Elsie's Business*.

You step forward. You reach up your coat sleeve, pull off your gold watch, and place it carefully on top of a ten pound bag of sugar. Step away. For Elsie. . . .

There are at least a hundred people, and the dance is slow. When it is done the drums give a final thump. The wicasa wakan *gathers the corners of the blanket together bagging the money in the middle, walks through the snow and hands it to you. Your arms are frozen at your sides.*

Native literature has never been a newcomer in the course of literary resistance to dominance. Natives have resisted discovery and political tyranny for centuries, from the first stories of contact and wily breach of trust in a monotheistic empire to the unbearable ironies of a constitutional democracy. The storiers of resistance are wise and tricky.

Keeshkemun, for instance, a nineteenth-century Anishinaabe storier and diplomat, teased a British military officer with tropes of natural reason and survivance. Keeshkemun created an avian sense of presence in a memorable riposte to military dominance. "I am a bird who rises from the earth, and flies far up, into the skies, out of human sight; but though not visible to the eye, my voice is heard from afar, and resounds over the earth."

N. Scott Momaday, Leslie Silko, Louis Owens, Diane Glancy, and many other novelists create animals and birds in dialogue and descriptive narratives by name, consciousness, metaphor, and allegory, which creates a natural sense of presence that overturns the monotheistic separation of humans and animals. The similes that favor humans over animals, or animal similes that demean and deprecate humans, are common in commercial literature.

"The imperial ravens stole my lunch. I was sitting on a bench in the park when a palace raven soared from the crown of the Ministry of Justice building and, with a perfect, silent dive, snatched the last piece of my bento sushi," writes Gerald Vizenor in *Hiroshima Bugi: Atomu 57*.

Tokyo was firebombed at the end of the war and the ravens quickly moved to the secure trees of the Imperial Palace. The more guttural ravens of the industrial areas, nearby docks, and remote sections of the city, resent the imperial strain, their haughty relatives, the palace ravens who survived the war as aesthetic victims.

The palace ravens search the restaurant trash at first light, and then, in smart teams, they raid the parks. By dusk they return to their roosts in the imperial sanctuary. My bento sushi became one of their stories of the day.

I watched the ravens descend at great speed from nearby buildings, a trace of silent black motion, a perfect flight, and snatch a cracker from a child, a rice cake from a schoolgirl, a sandwich from a tourist, with impunity and no moral responsibility. These ravens are a tribute to a criminal empire, the great, tricky warriors of Hibiya Park.

The narratives in this collection create an active sense of presence, a visionary motion of liberty, not an ethnical absence, and never an unseemly romantic levy of separatism, retreat, expiration, or the simulations of heroic tragedy. These stories and narratives repudiate the notion that literature is a cryptic representation of cultural victimry.

Literary theories pursue but seldom inspire stories or creative narratives by Native American Indians. Theories never anticipate innovative stories or narratives and never precede the clever, artistic variations of native storiers. Native narratives are literary art, and theories are translations or uncertain interpretations of that tensive union of memory, traces of convergence, tradition, culture, the tease, and irony of storiers.

Literary theory may provide the discourse to compare and construe the apparent evolution of literature, but the traces, tricky turns, and visionary reach of native narratives forever haunt the interpreters and translators. Some readers consider literature a mere representation of culture, and others observe the bloodline or reservation pedigree of the author as a source of authenticity. And some theorists have gone astray in the shadows of literary art, seduced by their own romantic imputations or reversions, deceived by the simulation of cultural representations and the ideologies of racialism advanced by the deniers of chance associations and survivance.

Native traditions are imagic instances of the actual creation in stories; natural reason; visual memories; dances; ceremonies;

and drawings on stone, bark, and sand. The occasions of native stories and the performances that actuated a sense of native presence were never mere liturgy.

Literary historians and theorists who endorse imperative representations of traditions to secure literature as liturgy ignore and, at times, inhibit the actual practices of literary art. The liturgical cruises into the native past divert and misrepresent the creative power of traditions, as if the practices of literary art were structural, an architectural concept that defines only the linguistic and material connections, an imperious declaration of academic sovereignty.

"I begin to think the books want me here. They want me to hear what they say. They talk from the written word," writes Diane Glancy in *Designs of the Night Sky*. "Maybe writing doesn't kill the voice. Put it in a grave. Maybe writing isn't the destroyer people think it is. . . . Sometimes I know the murmurings I hear are the voices struggling to cover themselves; to get out of the books. But where would they go?"

BLEED INTO ME

STEPHEN GRAHAM JONES

Captivity Narrative 109

Filius Nervosus

These Are the Names I Know

Bleed into Me

Discovering America

Captivity Narrative 109

His name was Aiche, like the letter. And all he ever meant to do that day was drive down to Great Falls and pawn the rifle, fold the ticket in a piece of plastic and hide it in his wallet for a couple of months. But things happen. Arson. Kidnapping. Gunplay. Aiche, stuck behind an early-morning school bus in residential, his truck too tall and too red to try swinging around. So he pulls forward each time the bus does, stops when it stops, watches the mothers bowl their children out into the yard and then stand there after the bus pulls away, their robes held tight to their throats. They stand there until there's nothing else they can do, and then they go in. Aiche nods at them in turn. The third one nods back, waves as she's already turning away. Aiche takes another drink of his coffee, and then another mother waves at him, holding her hand up long at the end, her arm slowing, eyebrows coming down. Aiche resettles his cup on the dash in what could be taken as a wave back, then rubs a smudge off the blue of the rifle by his leg, because he needs to get sixty dollars out of it. Four houses down, another robed woman waves at him, and now Aiche is burrowed down into the tall collar of his coveralls. One corner and six houses later is when it happens, when it starts happening: two children—eight, eleven—rolling off their front porch, aimed for the bus, the girl leading the boy across the two snows built up in their drive, the boy leaving perfect white breaths in the air, then looking up, pulling back at his sister's arm.

They look at the tall red Ford together, then back to the porch, and Aiche looks with them, to the mother, snapping her head away now, to the bus. It's rolling back, crunching through the slush. Aiche lets off his own brake, rolls back too—careful, careful—and the girl, her mitten already lifted for the door handle on that side of the truck, shakes her head like this is a game, like Aiche is playing with her. And then she gets it, the door. The wind fills the cab, sucking the steam from the coffee on the dash. Aiche has one hand on the wheel, the other on the shifter, and before he can do anything the two children are up, in. Looking at him. The straggly black hair. The skin.

"You're not Uncle Jay," the girl says.

Aiche shakes his head no, says it—*H*—and the mistake he makes is that, instead of touching the brake to stop rolling, he touches the gas, to ease back up to where he was. But it's like there's a chain between his truck and the bus, he's been following it for so many blocks now. When it pulls away, he's behind it, trying to look through his sliding back glass at the children's mother, still there.

"You're Indian," the girl says.

Aiche nods, asks her what school they go to.

She smiles—glitter on her lips—shakes her head. "Different ones," she says.

Aiche purses his lips, nods, nods. Drinks more of the coffee than he means to, just idling down the road now, still craning back for the children's mother. When he looks back in front of him, the bus is gone. Left, right, up. Behind him, the children's mother is standing on the porch again, the phone stretched out with her. Aiche closes his eyes and lets the clutch out, for the long roll downhill. Where the bus had to be going. Because this can still work.

"Here?" he says. "This way?"

The girl shrugs.

The boy isn't saying anything. When Aiche isn't shifting, he rests his hand on the scope of the rifle. He's going to tell the pawnshop owner that the scope alone is worth one-fifty. He drinks the coffee until it's gone and still there's no school, just a convenience store, standing up out of the road.

Aiche tells the girl to stay there, starts to close the door, then comes back for the gun. Because the boy's only eight.

He hooks the strap onto his right shoulder and leans into the glass door, gets two honey buns for the children, more coffee for himself, and sets it all on the counter. The clerk surrounds it with his hands, palm down, fingers spread. Aiche looks at them, looks at them, then follows the arms up to the clerk.

The rifle.

Aiche smiles, looks out to the blond heads of the two children, just there over the line of the dash, then turns back to the clerk.

"This isn't what you think," he says.

"And those are your kids," the clerk says. "I know the drill, man. Just take it easy."

"I'm trying to," Aiche says.

He leaves two dollar bills on the counter and gets into the truck again.

The girl flattens her voice out and tells him Aiche isn't his real name. That it's just a letter, that he's probably Horace or Harry or something.

Aiche nods, backs out, nods some more.

"Where's your school?" he asks her.

She takes him there with her index finger. They pull into the parents' lane. Someone in a sports jacket at the double doors of the gym waves at him, Aiche. At the truck. Aiche looks down at the girl.

"Can't you just take him with you?" he says—the boy.

"It's not his school," she says, then shuts the door hard enough that the ice caked on the glass calves off. Aiche ducks away from the clear view the man in the blazer has to have now, pulls down along the curb, into Great Falls. For legal purposes he tells the boy in as many ways as he can that he's not kidnapping him. The boy says he knows, he's been kidnapped once already, by his dad. His voice isn't shaking.

"Your dad?"

"He's in Arizona."

"Did he take you there?"

"No. We went to a hotel and watched cartoons and then called Mom."

"You know your phone number, don't you?"

The boy nods. Aiche smiles, asks the boy how he'd like to just go home today, skip school, take an Indian holiday? The boy shrugs, looks once at Aiche and then away. "The one with the Manimals," he says.

"What?"

"The cartoon."

"Oh."

"They have guns too."

And then the next thing happens. It's like driving into a mirror: Aiche pulls out of the parents' lane, into the school zone stretching two hundred feet in either direction, and coming at him in the road is his own tall red Ford, right down to the grill. Aiche rotates his head, watching the truck slip past.

Uncle Jay.

The only difference in the two trucks is that Uncle Jay has a red light on top of his cab, a power cable running from it into the door, down to the cigarette lighter. A volunteer fireman.

In Aiche's rearview mirror Uncle Jay slides sideways a bit, trying too hard to turn around. Aiche lets off the gas, to wait, but the truck behind him stops, and Uncle Jay steps down to lock the hubs. In his hands is another rifle.

Aiche looks over at the boy.

The boy's staring straight ahead.

Aiche tells him to put his seatbelt on.

"It is," the boy says.

"Good," Aiche says, and then they're driving as fast as the roads will let them, Uncle Jay a block behind, finally spinning out in some mother's yard, Aiche already coasting farther downhill, his coffee percolating into the vents of his defroster. The boy tells him he shouldn't say bad words. Aiche agrees, says he's sorry, and then noses the truck behind the double dumpsters of a thrift store, kills it. There's nothing to say, not really. Just Aiche, coming around to open the boy's door, guiding the boy down, leading him by the hand into the store, past the staring clerks and the secondhand lingerie to the back, where he can think. They stand there while he does, and finally he nods, asks the boy if he still knows his phone number. The boy nods. The pay phone is in the hall with the restrooms. Aiche dials the number the boy recites.

"Who are you?" the mother asks.

"He's okay," Aiche says.

"You can't just do this," she says.

"I'm going to leave him . . . " Aiche says, looking around, looking around, until he doesn't know the name of the place. He closes his eyes. ". . . Can't you just tell me where his school is?" he says, and when the mother starts crying he hangs up as gently as he can.

The boy's looking at him.

Aiche smiles.

"She said to buy you something," he says, and they do, a Manimal action figure from a bin—half man, half puma, with a looped string out his back to hold him by, or hang him with, something.

As they're crossing the parking lot, the boy reaches up for Aiche's hand, and then Aiche lights a match to the rag he cleaned the gun with last night, drops the rag in the dumpster. Because Uncle Jay is a fireman.

Four minutes later, they're back up in residential, Aiche out in the street looking for stadium lights, the kind that schools have. The picture of him that makes the paper the next morning is of him doing that, even: standing at the front of the truck, the rifle leaned across the hood, his right eye held close to the scope, his breath held in, so it won't fog up the lens.

Nothing, though. Just Uncle Jay, climbing the road behind them.

Getting back into the cab for the rest of the chase, Aiche looks north, to the reservation, to Browning, still four hours away, ten minutes of that town, five of that ten residential, and, in residential, six stop signs to slide through. At the second stop sign the near collision is a pale yellow house, because they have to make the downhill turn, and at the fourth the near collision is another red truck, Uncle Jay. The locked hubs of Uncle Jay's truck pop like gunfire as he turns wide in the rearview, roostertailing through a lawn.

Aiche starts smiling like it hurts.

"What's your name?" he asks the boy, but the boy doesn't answer, and over the next two miles he tells the boy everything he knows—about sneaking into Glacier with his grandfather to hunt, how they just shot an old moose who wouldn't leave them alone; about the time his best friend in junior high stood out in the road by Starr School all day once, trying to get run over, just to go somewhere else; about how his cousin Natt in Seattle only robs places with water guns, because you don't get in as much trouble if you don't have bullets; about how his plan this morning had been simple—to pawn the rifle and pay back the gas money he had to borrow to get to Great Falls in the first place; about how he thought all this land they were driving through maybe used to be Prickly Pear Valley or something, a long time ago. The boy watches the yellow grass whip by, asks if they're going to a motel room like last time, and Aiche looks out the window with him, out to where the grass is still in relation to them, a fixed point.

"You're supposed to be in school today," he says, "right?"

"Indian holiday," the boy says back, quiet.

Aiche smiles his best tragic smile, nods, and takes his right foot off the accelerator, coasting to a stop. Uncle Jay does the same, blocking the road fifty yards closer to Great Falls. Aiche tells the boy who doesn't have a name that he's sorry, and then the wood stock of the gun is in his hand.

The boy asks Aiche if he's going to turn into a wolf now.

Aiche looks at him, looks at him.

"A wolf?" he says, and then sees, gets it: Manimals, Indians.

He shrugs, looks back to Uncle Jay, says maybe, yeah.

Through Uncle Jay's scope—his rifle eased into the crotch of his door and cab—all there can be is an Indian of some kind, a nephew kidnapped at gunpoint. Motion in the cab, for too long, an action figure getting left behind on the dash, and then the door opening, the nephew on the Indian's knees, the Indian holding the rifle barrel up, its butt against hip bone.

They step down as one.

The Indian keeps the rifle well away from his body, the nephew on his other arm. He stares at Jay, says something that doesn't carry, and then sends the nephew walking over, looking back once and getting waved on for it. Whatever the Indian's saying, he says it again, and this time points, back to where a dumpster is billowing black smoke up into the sky. Like that should be enough.

Aiche. That was his whole name, like the letter.

And already, then, he was pulling away in second gear, picking the action figure off the dashboard, looping it over his rearview mirror so that it blocked the highway patrolmen converging behind him, pulling him over for Driving While Indian, more or less, but unable in the end to charge him with anything worth the ride back into town because the rifle he'd carried onto school grounds and then used on a convenience store clerk had no shells the troopers could find, shells they begged and bargained existence for, tried to dig out of ashtrays and door panels and headliners and every other possible place except for the pockets of my school jeans as I walked from one red truck to another, moving between letters, the smoke marking my return, leading me deeper into town than I ever wanted to go.

Filius Nervosus

1

Men at forty are above the law; my father carries nunchakus to the grocery store. He says he learned them in Vietnam, before he started carrying a briefcase. He was sixteen in 1975; he's never been out of the country. In his high school yearbook he's often caught with plaid pants, a dubious cigarette in his off hand, real casual. Those pants are in my closet, brown and orange. My father was thinner than me at seventeen, but the pants, I can't help myself sometimes. The flared legs swish against each other, up one aisle of the convenience store, down the next. Against a plaid wall I'm invisible from the waist down. I come home with a Slurpee, and over a dinner of mashed potato sandwiches my father tells me that if I ever have to kill anyone, to do it calmly, because if I do it in anger, then a calm me somewhere down the line will feel remorse. It's the psychology of warfare, he says, tearing, chewing.

I went to the army surplus store the other day, just to look around.

The police watch me.

2

All my mother's stories are permutations of the same tired memory: there she is, a mythical seven years old. Backyard. Birthday party, sometimes hers, sometimes my uncle's. Her father who used to watch all the movies has this great idea for all the kids to write down their wishes on little fortune-cookie strips of paper. They do, brows furrowed, elbows furious. Behind them the older generation drinks helium from balloons and talks with a limited roadrunner vocabulary. But there's enough balloons left where nobody has to share. Each of the cousins ties their strip to a balloon. My grandfather is crying and smoking a cigarette to try and hide it, and then in a swirl of motion and extended fingers the balloons are off, the wishes going heavenward, everyone's eyes primitive white and staring.

This is where my mom gets that thing with her voice that she thinks is irony but is really more of an excuse for the pattern of her life. She'll splash some coffee over the edge of her cup so I won't see her cheeks flush and then say that her little-girl wish was just that she wanted her balloon back.

My father does his chucks in the backyard and she makes grocery lists for him, impossible lists that require remote freezer sections on the wrong side of town. She tried to teach me to dance the hustle the other night but we were both trying to hide that we were drunk and it was all wrong.

I keep my wishes in the ashtray of my father's car, because nobody smokes anymore.

3

Friday my father says his secretary's having a garage sale. I know her address, find the ad in the paper. Big block letters: ABORTION GARAGE SALE. Everything must go. No early birds. We get there at seven o'clock and the cars are already lined up. Mostly feminine cars, my dad notes, putting on his aviation shades.

We approach and conversation dies. A haggle stops midway through and money changes hands prematurely. I pick through old vinyl like I recognize any of the names. I do my eyebrows in subdued surprise at finding whatever record it is I'm pretending to look for. My father works his way in in circles, securing the perimeter first, as is his style. He's brought one of my mother's canvas shopping bags for the occasion. He inserts ashtrays and bookends seemingly at random, decorating some diner or halfway house from his youth. I've got an armful of records. He does his chin like *let's go,* so I follow him to the secretary with the fanny pack who absolutely refuses to smile. She looks in his bag, at my records that are marked twenty-five cents, five for a dollar. My father offers her three crisp one-hundred-dollar bills. She shakes her head, calls him by his first name and says, "Not enough."

We return to the tables and racks. In an umbrella bucket I find an imitation katana, carved plastic grip, thirty-inch steel blade. Still though, the center of balance is right. My father's unshaven face breaks into a grin. It costs us five hundred dollars to get out of there.

4

That night we sit in the backyard under the droplight and I watch my father's whetstone make little circles on the blade like he can wash it sharp. Three times my nameless friend has honked out front, three times I've not been able to leave. Inside, my mother is still feeding the Lhasa apso we got her on the way back from the garage sale, four and a half pounds of apology. I expect the dog to keel over any moment. Me and my father call it Spaz, try not to notice it the rest of the time.

A week drags on, then another.

My father calls from the office and tells me about wind shear and parachuting from low altitudes into wet climates. He says I might need this information. But I don't even have a war to pretend I was in. I listen, make noises like I'm taking notes in my head but really I'm balancing the katana on the palm of my hand, straight up. It's like a piece of me now. After dinner each night my father and me stroll out to the backyard and he takes week-old cantaloupes from the trunk of his car. He lobs them like a softball at my back, and in a single motion I turn, swing, and the two halves fall to the ground.

It's a beautiful thing.

5

One morning before school I wake to find my mother in her house robe, in the kitchen. She's cooking bacon, all of it. She's crying. She tells me the same old story. My father's already off to work. It's just her and the dog and me, and I'm almost gone too. "Watch this," she says, like it might keep me there. She holds the bacon up at waist level and the dog springs up and takes a neat bite. "Yeah," I say. "No, no, *watch*," she says, then holds the bacon at breast level. The dog takes a neat bite, lands softly. Then she holds it over her head, and because I imagine the dog cocking its four-inch legs and flying right past her—because I imagine it becoming small in the sky, leaving us far behind—I drop my toast, a necessary distraction.

The dog waddles over, wide as it is long, a pufferfish, twin black nostrils blowing.

My mother dabs her eyes with the belt of her robe and tells me to call my father, she needs him to pick something up on the way home from work. I try to explain that he's not even there yet, there's no way, but still I have to dial the numbers and listen to it ring and ring. When she finally turns her back I'm already down at the convenience store in my trench coat, the katana on a rope slung over my shoulder.

I pay full price for my Slurpee because I'm a decent person.

But I don't have to.

6

The day my mother sends my father for a seedless yellow-meat out-of-season watermelon we have to pick him up from jail. She says he's had it coming to him for a long time; he doesn't say anything. There are nunchaku impressions on the left side of his face, though, meaning whichever shopper or stockboy he intimidated was right-handed. He taught me to take note of these type of things. He doesn't have the watermelon. They get in a fight about it. We have to stop at the martial arts supply store on the way home, for more chucks. I step out of the car there and keep walking, finally get to the secretary's house. The garage sale remains, the innards of her house smeared all over the lawn. I ask her how she's feeling. She says maybe she shouldn't be talking to me, and I tell her don't worry, it's not a genetic thing, really: I'm not like my dad.

Over egg sandwiches she tells me in raw, clinical terms about the procedure she's had visited upon her, and uses lots of peach-pitting analogies so I can really understand. I ask her where my father was going after work. She cocks her head and says that grocery store over on Magnolia, why?

"No reason," I say, and when I'm hiding behind the dumpster in our alley hours later I don't know who to blame, my mother for sending my father in search of impossible items, or my father for believing an impossible item could possibly smooth everything over.

The grocery store on Magnolia calls two days later to schedule an interview, but I fail the bag-boy questions in ways that cause the assistant manager to leave the door to his office open, where people can see us.

7

My father doesn't speak to us for four days, until his face is almost healed, and then he takes it out on the sapling out back, spinning the chucks deep into the night. He's taken to calling everyone Charlie under his breath, so my mother keeps her distance. By the toolshed now there's a whole truckload of seedless yellow-meat watermelons. Sometimes when I'm standing in the yard looking at the tree he'll still lob one my way, and it'll die, and we'll have that. Spaz licks the rinds clean somehow, his tongue like a horse's, as long as his short body. I hear it and my mother in the early mornings, playing their jump-higher-and-higher game, the dog's landing not so soft anymore. It shakes the whole house. If my father slept more than four hours at a time, it'd wake him. But he's on watch.

When it happens is on Good Friday.

It's after school and I'm standing in the backyard staring at the sapling, trying to establish something, a connection or a communion or just a shared shadow. My mother's talking to my father's secretary on the phone, pretending she's a siding peddler. She doesn't know anything about siding. Yesterday it was bibles and guilt. Since she found my garage sale records under the bed she plays them all the time, the globe light over the linoleum floor like a disco ball, light dancing off stove handles and coffee percolators.

And me, I'm standing there, tense, ready for anything, and then I hear it: something whistling through the air, something heavy, almost to my back. I turn, swing effortlessly, and Spaz falls in two pieces to the ground. The distinct smell of bacon grease. My mother dropping the phone. I stand there in my stiff plaid pants, trying to blend with the foliage, and stand there for hours, until my father comes in the front door and their screaming starts, neither taking the blame for me this time. Nobody wants to be guilty. I've given them that at least, to share. Finally my father's magazine collection comes spilling out the bedroom window, my mother's red fingernails just behind them, withdrawing now, and in the silence I know my father is sitting down somewhere, trying to contain himself, his fists at the sides of his head. But he can't. He appears at the door, the chucks held low and limber at his thigh. He thinks he can get away with anything. The air thickens and warms between us, my father's chucks dancing silent across his back, belly, neck, and shoulders until they blur into perfection. I look through them with my face slack as my unborn brother's—acquiring shorthand through the uterine wall, his room decorated with castoff ashtrays and bookends—and then I bring the katana down cleanly, severing the cord, setting us adrift in the lawn, a father and son in a decaying orbit, circling with knees properly bent until all metaphor breaks down and we have to see each other as we are—naked, bleeding down the back of our faces, fighting for what we think is our lives, what we think our lives should be. What they aren't. This is the art of war. We lean into it together, my mother watching through the frosted glass of the kitchen, touching our refracted images with only the tips of her fingers, as if we might shatter into a thousand pieces. We do anyway.

These Are the Names I Know

A Bird

We were eight and nine when you found the bird baby dying, dried up in the sun. I told you all about how the momma would never take it back if she smelled us on it, but since you were older and maybe since there were black ants all crawling in the bird baby's mouth already, we took it with us, in the pocket of my shirt close to my heart, where it could stay warm, and I spit love in its mouth once when you weren't looking, because that's how they eat.

Two days later when the bird baby was living and dying finally in a shoebox under your bed, we were out looking for bugs to crush in the eyedropper and I found that spotted eggshell, cut clean in half by maybe a momma bird's beak working from the outside, maybe from a baby bird's working from inside, maybe together. Either way, you said it was the only one you had ever seen and it had to mean something, had to be more than just a shell; you said it was a sign, finding a bird baby and then its shell like that, and it meant the bird was ours, and because I was a girl you wouldn't listen to anything I said, all you could see was you with this bird, how it would look someday.

So I quit talking then, just like that, that easy, fourteen and a half days nobody heard me say a word, not until I had to sit in the office all day waiting for my mom to get off work to come ask me what was wrong and yell at the principal that I was his fault, that I wasn't like this at home, I never shut up then, always talking. She was lying like always, and when she went out to her car for a cigarette I told the principal she was a liar and then I told him some about the bird baby but not all, just about how me and you had seen it, and he held his finger to his lips when my mom came back smelling like smoke and they sat and listened and when I finally ran out of things to say I started making things up about jobs I would never have and people I would never meet and somewhere in the middle of it all I wound up crying through dinner that night thinking about that bird baby under your bed, the little fingers of a yellow lightbulb feeling down through the pencil holes in the box, the sound of you sleeping in the sky above, waiting for everything like it was all going to come to you so right and so perfect.

A Mouse

One job I never had was at a warehouse full of seed. All the warehouses together went something like fourteen acres of covered concrete, no air conditioning, old brick walls that kept it cool even in the summer, brick walls that had people's names carved into them that went back to 1954 and then some. My name was Ring then and I was an eighteen-year-old boy that even the army didn't want, and the way I carved my sign was by drawing a circle, which was good for a while up there above the phone, at least until Reginald put two eyes and a mouth in the middle and made a face out of me.

He quit before I could get him back right, but not before he told me once after work that he had been married years gone by and had lost his wife to cancer in the bone so deep nobody could get it out, and he was raising his little girl back at his trailer alone now, praying hard every night she wouldn't die the same way, but knowing she would just the same.

All he ever ate too was potted meat and Vienna wieners from the can, and even though I was always hungry back then, I never did share any of his food like he wanted me to, even though he said it'd let me grow a mustache like a real man.

The day before he left is the day I think about the most. Him and me were out in warehouse nine, where we kept the better part of our corn, and we were walking around with big soft blocks of camphor, cutting flakes off here and there and leaving them where we thought they'd best keep the rats out. Sometime maybe around six everybody started leaving; we could hear their trucks and Danny's ratty Harley. Me and Reginald were making our way to the dock door trying to get rid of the last of the camphor in big obvious chunks when somebody shut and locked the door not knowing about us, and we both knew without saying it that we were there for the night.

I didn't think it was all that bad, being clocked in fourteen more hours, and had just started arranging bags of treated pink corn for a bed of sorts when I heard Reginald beating on the door with a shovel at the other end of the warehouse, and it was then I remembered about his little girl—maybe Audrey was her name—and I helped him and we tried every door and even broke the skinny glass window out of two of them, but it was no good.

By the time the sun was all done with leaking in the loose places where the walls met the ceiling I couldn't even be around Reginald anymore. I tried though, for a bit, but every time I said anything to him he started shaking around his mouth, so finally I just went back to my corn bed and was lying there burning matches one by one when I saw, half in, half out of one of my bags, a poisoned dead mouse the size of my thumbnail, its skin pulled tight around the bones, eyes gone, teeth bigger than I ever saw, bigger than they should have been, and I started shaking then like Reginald, not really for his little girl back at his trailer waiting for him to get home, but for Reginald himself, for how he ate his potted meat off the end of the same popsicle stick every day and then shut that stick up in foil and put it in the refrigerator to keep the cancer germs out.

Tin foil and cold. That was all it took.

He never died.

A Frog

Nighttime and our only child is still never born. We sit. We sit together on the couch, opposite ends, me with my books about history, you with yours. Outside it's the rain dying down finally, yellow headlights sometimes on the backside of the drapes, sometimes not. This night while you're asleep on the couch I'll sit arranging the magnets on the refrigerator until three, and in the morning when you wake you won't be able to read the message I've left in the plasticoated symbols trailing up out of blue Louisiana like Lewis and Clark. I too will have forgotten what I meant to say, but the feeling will remain. And I'll be driving. The Cascades. The Sierras.

This night though. Now. Three sets of headlights ago you lit your last cigarette and now you've forgotten it, and I start to cry down the back of my face about things we should be remembering: a bowl in the garage. The smoke gathers around the only lamp in the room and forces the shadows into a tortured dance. The wall is silent. I open the sliding glass door to breathe the after-rain air and close my eyes, see the mountains and the road climbing them. Going to the Sun Road, like in the paper Montana on the map in the glove compartment somewhere.

"Close the door," you say, the air, the air, and I see your hand has found again its cigarette stub. As you breathe in, the ember glows deep under the crusted ash and I see your face once more, see it all at once, in every way I've known you: as a twelve-year-old with hands full of lice and mites and power; as a boy-man looking across the bench seat of your father's truck at me, the dome light making you soft and pale beautiful; as a voice on the other end of the line promising me how good things are, saying it over and over, pleading it into existence; as a sunglassed stranger standing over an abbreviated plot of ochered earth and rubbing the slacks between your fingers because you only want to be somewhere else, anywhere else, never try again; here. The beer, the bourbon, the ice falling silently on the cream carpet to melt into a world of diaphanous trees.

Oh God.

I don't close the door. I leave it open and feel you behind me. I leave it open until the frogsong comes rolling across the shiny pasture into our childless home. *They're praying*, I whisper, where you can't hear me unless you try. They're praying, their voices all together in some desperate plea for more, more, wanting only to drown once and for all in the warm wetness of the pond, that soft second womb where the flies dance higher and higher.

Your eyes bore into the small of my back, where I can still feel you.

"What're you doing?" you ask.

"The frogs," I say.

"The frogs," you say back.

In some places they rain down out of the sky. People have recorded this.

You laugh through your nose but still I don't close the door. Instead I stand there between two worlds and I wait.

And Five Arrows

This it remains.

Three months after you told my dad I was pregnant and he had given us forty-eight dollars in bottled change and shown us the door. Silver and copper and telephone poles fused together with words. I was twenty-one and you were a year older. We were legal. We were running. We were outside Phoenix Arizona, in the flat of a pasture by some little motel-room cabin that we wound up never paying for, even though it was by the week and we were there for four. It was the closest we came to a honeymoon. My mother had given us a parqueted wooden bowl where we separated the dimes from the nickels from the lint. The sun went down every day.

The last of our gas money had just turned into a red fiberglass bow in your hands, and we were out in the pasture with a handful of arrows testing it out against anything that looked worthy.

After a while I was lying down on that blanket we had, trying to talk to you about names. I was saying them all from my book: Abe, Ainge, Alan, Amon, Ash, and then on into the *B*s. You knew it was going to be a boy, had to be, wouldn't even listen to the girl names, but that was back when you would even talk about it, before we found Seattle and the rain.

I was all the way into the *L*s when you started in talking, talking like you were talking to yourself, like I wasn't even there, talking about us being married, living in a house with a dog and maybe even another kid after this one and some neighbors to have cookouts with, and I lay there and listened and I cried hearing you say those things because they were so right, so perfect, so like everything I ever wanted, and you kept talking and talking and after a while I quit really listening to what you were saying.

Sixteen years later though, I can still hear you. I'm still on that blanket with Abe Ainge Alan Amon Ash six months along in my stomach and never going to die, never. I can still hear you, still see you, still believe you. You're leaned back against the azure sky like a Greek statue, shooting arrows straight up. Three of them are buried nose first about fifteen feet out from the edge of my blanket, and you're talking out loud about what kind of car you might want to drive to your work, what kind of work you might want, and you're telling me you'll buy all watermelon stuff for the kitchen like I've always wanted and now another arrow is in the air going up, up, and I'm here on the blanket waiting and waiting and when the arrow disappears I close my eyes and your voice carries me.

Bleed into Me

And then there was the brother (me) who didn't know what to do at the funeral, so just stood there exactly four paces from his brother's casket, following the pattern in the carpet with the toe of his borrowed black shoe. In the inside pocket of the suit jacket he was wearing was the carnation some uncle or cousin had probably meant to pin to a prom date once, years ago. The last time the suit had been worn.

His brother in the casket was waxy and fixed. There were lines in his hair where the comb had dragged through. They must have had to sit him up for that, one person's hands between his shoulder blades, holding him, the other with the comb always in her hands, never between her teeth.

The brother with his toe in the carpet closed his eyes. His father brushed his hand as he passed, dragging smoke in from the porch, crushing his cigarette into the glass ashtray.

"You okay?" he asked.

And then there was the father who didn't know what to say, or how.

The brother shrugged, watched the smoke from the dying cigarette trail up into the parchment lampshade. On the porch on the way in he had stopped to look back at the waiting hearse, and his hand had followed a post up to a support beam, and then he had followed the lip of the support beam to the door. It was a straight line but for one thing: just before the door there was a fleshy lump in the lip of the beam. The brother kept his hand there, swinging to the left some to let an aunt pass, his hanging tie brushing her shoulder, and when he was alone he pulled his hand down. The fleshy lump was a fishing lure, a soft glow-in-the-dark worm, only some prior mourner had run two stick pins in through the face, longways. The pins had pearly heads, were eyes. He didn't know what he had thought the worm was going to be. He put it back, entered the funeral home, approached the casket then backed off four paces to the side, holding his hands one over the other before him.

Everyone was pretending the small green dumpster tucked into the back of the parking lot was just another dumpster. Everyone was eating donuts and laughing with their whole face. The brother started over with his toe, the carpet.

The day after his brother died he had found in his brother's glove compartment an envelope of photographs of the two of them as children, and it wasn't good. He made himself look at each one, though, until he'd placed the season, the year, their age, the photographer. The glue on the envelope had been used up but the backs of the photographs were still tacky from the album his brother had peeled them from at three in the morning, hunched over in the hall, the front door open so that he could flit away the moment their mother's bedcovers rustled, then hide in the bushes all night guarding the house, his pockets full of silverware and heirlooms and pawn receipts, the open front door locked as if he'd meant to pull it shut behind him, then couldn't afford the sound.

In the car on the way to the funeral home the mother had read aloud every street sign and billboard they passed. "Was that it?" she asked, about the street the funeral home wasn't on, slipping behind them. The mother who didn't recognize her own town anymore. The brother who was still getting used to the borrowed suit had shrugged. He had had the headlights on at first, then pushed the knob back in, off. Then on.

One morning he had found one of his dead brother's cigarettes smoldering into the front porch, and he had picked it up for a last drag then dropped it instead, rolled it underfoot. Another time he caught his brother ducking out over the front mat at daybreak, and the two of them fought hard on the dewed-up lawn with their parents and neighbors watching, and the whole time the dead brother was holding one of their mother's gilt-edged plates, and it never broke, and the brother ran backwards down the street with it glinting in the sunlight, his arms out, nose bleeding around his smile, shoulders lifted in apology. Ten months later his whole face would be bleeding from a skull fracture, and his little brother would hold his head in his lap under a guttering dome light with the broken-open face towards his stomach and say all kinds of things he never knew he had had words for, things like *don't worry, it'll be all right, just let it all out, I'm sorry.*

It would be at the high school parking lot, all the trucks circled around for the headlights, and there would be a senior cornerback from another town sitting on the not-yet-dead brother's chest, an unlikely chunk of asphalt held over his head, ready to bring down for the third time, the time that would push the two of them into legend—how the one on top didn't want to do it, how the one on his back wouldn't say he'd had enough. And wouldn't, and wouldn't. And he would live through that and more, too—every way there was to die in Martin County, like he was looking for them—and still show up at the house at three in the morning, to stand in the dark living room and ask himself *what now?*

Once it was the rosewood desk, tied upside down to the roof of a long-hooded car.

Another time it was the condenser unit for the air conditioner.

Towards the end—when he was more a rumor than a brother—it was the plastic forks and spoons left floating in the dishwater; the long copper wire that ran from the antenna to the television set; the fake jewelry his mother had started leaving out for him, closer and closer to his old room.

When he took the desk, he left the stapler and hole punch and paper clip cup on the carpet exactly as his mother had had them on the desk.

That next night his mother hid the gun from the men of the house. Because they would protect her. Even against him. In his eyes in the photographs you can even see it a little. That he was already sorry for everything he was going to do. That his mother and father and brother weren't supposed to miss the cutlery and the wedding bands and the rest, but the photographs. And nobody said it at the funeral but the brother standing in the borrowed suit knew that he was only there because his dead brother had been bad enough for both of them, taken it on himself, and in thanks he drew the cigarette up from the glass ashtray, trying to breathe the end red again, then pocketed the ashtray too.

And then there was the mother who hadn't seen the envelope of photographs yet, who wasn't yet ready to see them. After the funeral when she wasn't wasn't *wasn't* thinking about her son in the ground in his box with the earth baked hard over it like a shell. But one day the shell cracked open, and her son came back. It was three in the morning all night long; things were disappearing again.

At first it was the new set of steak knives, removed one by one from the wooden block she had long ago super-glued at the proper angle to the countertop. Then it was her hair rollers, and then the extra belt for the vacuum cleaner, and then her husband couldn't find the remote one evening, and she knew. Without being told, she knew.

She said his name when no one was in the room, and then with darkness would rush everyone away from the television, off to bed. Once she sat at her missing desk—the stapler and the

Rolodex and the lamp all arranged on the carpet in the arc that made the most sense—but then made herself get up; *live*. Because he needed her. She wanted to breastfeed him again, to hold his head to her like that.

"You okay?" her husband asked, and she nodded yes, yes, her uncurled hair falling over her eyes, then disappeared for hours at a time during the day, haunting the pawnshops as only a mother can, inspecting each can opener and doorstop, looking for her son in their curved reflections, their familiar heft. She found her college typewriter at a junk shop on the industrial side of town, and walked out with it cradled in her arms. The warehouses stood solemn around her, in respect.

At a secondhand clothing store that smelled of mothballs and teeth left to dry overnight she found a strand of her pearls in a shoebox spilling over with plastic earrings and dead watches. They were real, the pearls; she talked the clerk down to a dollar-fifty, then forced ten dollars on him, then just emptied her purse on the counter. But it still wasn't enough: her son wasn't eating the food she left on the kitchen table for him. He was going to starve like that.

The household items she recovered she placed in the living room, the kitchen, the entry hall. It was like going back in time.

After two nights without dinner, her son and husband crept into the kitchen at three in the morning, gorged themselves on the food left there and never talked about it.

When the mother's typewriter disappeared again, she left in its place a new ribbon, and then it was gone as well. She followed it all over town: from the pawnshop on Eighth to the one nestled between all the bail bondsmen on Francis Street, by the tracks. All the pawnshop men were the same, too: leather vests, untended sideburns, faces bisected by vertical bars. And they all remembered her dead son, had all just seen him.

Once, leaving the pawnshop on Francis, she passed the boy who had helped steal her rosewood desk. She cinched her scarf around her chin and followed him and followed him, all the glass of his car still shattered from the weight of the desk on the roof. He wasn't going anywhere, though. Just driving.

At a pay phone she called her husband to ask if he was there, maybe—her dead son—and her husband didn't answer, didn't know what to say. That he was hungry.

That was the night she crouched in the bushes, guarding the house. Her plan was to let him in, then close the door behind him.

He must have seen her though, crept past.

And it wasn't because he didn't love her. She was his *mother.* It was because he couldn't help it. Because he had friends who got out of jail and just drove and drove.

Her husband carried her in the next morning. There were old cigarette butts all around her like ash. After that she couldn't leave the house anymore, but three in the morning was still there for her, for all of them, and she would tie her bathrobe around her waist with the knot that made the most sense and her husband would walk ahead of her through the house, hiding the valuables, rearranging them, and her son who was still wearing the borrowed suit would crouch outside each window to catch what she dropped out—the hair dryers and quilts and baking sheets of their life—and he was still smoking the same cigarette his brother had left, watching the window he was under with one eye, the street with the other.

And then there was the father who would always remember his dead son like this: walking up the sidewalk at five years old in moonboots, each of his footsteps timed perfectly with some roofer's nail gun. It was like he was a giant; the father had been changing the oil then, hidden under their old car.

This was years before he ever had to hold a gun on anybody in the living room and mean it. Years before he had to sit in emergency room after emergency room with his wife, telling his youngest son that he did good, he did fine, there was nothing else he could have done. He was slick with blood, though, the son. Trying to read a magazine.

The first thing the father did after the funeral was get a different job, and then a different job, and then a different one after that. He was a security guard and a customer service operator for a video game company and a parachute packer. But none of them lasted. During the day he filled out applications and watched the sky, to see if people would fall from it or float. After the video game company fired him he bought the game at one of his wife's pawnshops and called customer service with questions that always came down not to *how*, but *why?*

He thought he might like to work at a lube shop. Or a zoo. But then he became a roofer, until the roof collapsed out from under him one day and he fell for a moment into some other family's life. They were in the living room building something complicated but magical from popsicle sticks. The two fathers stood looking at each other, and the lesser turned, walked out.

The reason the roof collapsed was a young boy had been walking up the street, and the father had gunned a nail into the shingles with each step the boy took, until the boy was past and there was a creaking half moon of embedded nail heads before the father's knees.

He fell through and didn't stop falling for days, and when he stood it was into another job, writing fortune cookies. It didn't last. He grew his sideburns out and tried to hire on at a pawnshop, but they could tell right away what stage of grief he was in. To prove them wrong he hung from the steel bars of their windows until the sirens came. One of the fortunes that had gotten him fired was that when a father is walking around the house with his dead son, the wife is the only one who can take him away. It had no rhyme, though, the floor boss said, no *reason*, but that was the whole point.

That afternoon the father found a glass ashtray on his workbench. It had been polished for hours. He appreciated that and sat watching it, the vent hood for the kitchen range pushing all his wife's cooking into the garage. It was almost like eating.

He walked the zoo, looking at the animals.

He walked the backyard, watched his formally dressed son steal his mother's typewriter. They looked at each other across the wild grass, and then the son eased out the gate, slipped down the alley.

Nobody ever got anything out of pawn in this family. They always had to buy everything twice, three times, more. The father smiled to himself: *more*.

He tried getting a job as caretaker at the cemetery, but they could see he was still grieving too, and that he didn't have any references. He stood over his son's grave for hours anyway, tending it with his shadow, no pay. One afternoon he stole everyone else's flowers—real and fake—and placed them at his son's headstone by color, but the next morning they were gone again.

"Something's wrong here," he said to himself.

His oldest son was dead. That was what was wrong.

He dug the old moonboots out of the garage and left them on the grave, but then his wife brought them home the next week, from the salvage store. His oldest son rustled when he walked, each pocket of his suit choked with flower petals.

The father wanted a parachute too, like other people had. Or to fall through another roof, into a house he *knew*, a living room not piled with items his wife was remembering from a life they'd never lived: shoe buffers, boxes of fire alarms, mirrors with the backing peeled away so you could see the wall behind them.

One morning he found pictures of his two sons arranged in chronological order on the kitchen table, and then the phone rang, and his remaining son was in jail. He had been riding around with one of his dead brother's old friends; they had been looking for a desk.

On the way home the father asked his son for career advice. His son offered him a cigarette. He took it, smoked with one elbow out the window—the son the same, just with the opposite elbow—and remembered the emergency room that time with all the blood. The way the magazine kept slipping from his son's hands.

He wanted to work at a lube shop because he wanted to be under cars again, to be changing oil again, to see the world as a horizontal stripe again, one his dead son could walk up out of. He was too old, though. And cried too much. They didn't tell him that but he knew.

"You should be a comedian," his remaining son had told him minutes after he had asked for career advice, right before they got to their garage. A comedian. So the father walked down the street away from the lube shop trying to make up a joke. Because the world was a funny place. To prove it, a long car drove by with no windows and a beautiful rosewood desk balanced upside down on its roof, two dim shapes in the front seat, their arms out the window trying to hold the desk down.

The father smiled for the first time in weeks.

And then there was the father who lost his son, he said, already gathering speed after the car, so he got a job as an animal handler, just to feel the chimps' hands laced behind his neck, and the street roared with laughter and he ran through it carrying his dead son in his arms, holding his broken face to his stomach, telling him like his other son had that night in the high school parking lot that it would be all right, he could just bleed into him, he would save it all.

Discovering America

Because I'm Indian in Tallahassee Florida the girl behind the counter feels compelled to pull the leather strap ($1.19 per foot) around her neck, show me her medicine pouch, how authentic it is. "Yeah," I say, "hmm," and don't tell her about the one-act play I'm writing, about this Indian in the gift shop at the bottom of Carlsbad Caverns. His name isn't Curio but that's what the lady calls him when she sighs into line with her Germanic accent and her Karl May childhood. "You should do a rain dance or something," she tells him, she's never seen heat like this, like New Mexico. In the play she's sweating, he's sweating, and there's uncounted tons of rock above them, all this pressure.

In Tallahassee it rained all the time.

I stayed there for eleven months, nineteen days, and six hours.

Because I'm Indian at a party in Little Rock Arkansas, a group of students approaches me out of a back room of the house, ceremony still thick on their breath. In a shy voice their leader asks me what kind of animal my spirit helper is, and when I can't quite get enough tact into my mouth to answer, they make a show of respect, say they understand if I can't tell them, really. They tell me theirs, though: a grasshopper, a dragonfly, three wolves, and somewhere in there I become that tall, silent Indian in Thomas Pynchon's "Mortality and Mercy in Vienna," right before he goes cannibalistic in the middle of an otherwise happening party. The working title of the play I'm still writing is *The Time That Indian*

Started Killing Everybody, and standing there with my beer I don't revise it.

In Little Rock there were all kinds of bugs I hadn't seen before.

I stayed there for five months, four days, and twenty-two hours.

Because I'm Indian in Odessa Texas the guy who picks me up off the side of the road asks me what kind. He's an oilfield worker. His dashboard is black with it. When I say *Blackfeet* he finishes for me with *Montana*, says yeah, he drilled up there for a while. Cold as hell. "Yeah," I say, thinking this is going to be an all right ride. He drives and tells me how when he was up there he used to ride a helicopter to the rig every morning, it was *that* cold. In trade I tell him how the National Guard had to airlift hay and supplies a couple of winters back. He nods as if this is all coming back to him, and then, with both arms draped over the wheel real casual, asks me if they still run over Indians up there? I turn to him and he explains the sport, even hangs a tire into the ditch to show me how it's done.

In Odessa the butane pumps go all night, and it's hard to sleep.

I stayed there for three months, fourteen days, and fourteen hours.

Because I'm Indian the guys at the warehouse in Clovis New Mexico add a single feather to the happy face that's been carved into the back of my locker ever since I got there. It's not like looking in a mirror. Every time it's not like looking in a mirror. My second week there we're sweeping rat droppings into huge piles, and when I lean over one to see what Butch is pointing at he slams his broom down, drives it all into my face. That weekend I start coughing it all up, become sure it's the hantavirus that's been killing Indians all over. My whole check goes into the pay phone, calling everyone, talking to them one last time, reading them my play, the part where Curio kills one of the gift-shop people the old way, which means he hits him across the face with a log of Copenhagen, then follows him down to finish it, out of mercy.

In Clovis they don't turn their trucks off so you can talk on the phone, so you have to scream.

I stayed there for four weeks, one day, and two and a half hours.

Because I'm Indian in Carlsbad New Mexico the crew I'm working with calls me Chief, motions me over every time there's another animal track in the dirt. "I don't know," I tell them about the tracks, even though I do, and for a couple of hours we work in silence, up one row, down another. Once I find strange and cartoonish tracks in my row—traced with the sharp corner of a hoe—but I pretend to miss them, pretend no one's watching me miss them. All this pretending. Towards the end of the day I pass one of the crew and, without looking up, he asks if I've scalped anybody today, Chief? I unplant a weed from his row, look up for the briefest moment, long enough to say it: "Nobody you know." He doesn't laugh, and neither do I, and then later that night in a gas station I finish the play I started writing in Florida. It starts when the clerk wipes the sweat from his forehead, says how damn hot it is. And dry. I neither nod nor don't nod, just wait for him to say it.

In Carlsbad New Mexico the law is sluggish, slow to respond.

I stay there for sixteen hours, nine minutes, and fifty-two seconds, and when the rain comes it's not because I danced it up, but because I brought it with me.

MENDING SKINS

ERIC GANSWORTH

Prologue: *Opening Addresses*

Border One: *Burying Voices*

Border Two: *Burning Memories*

Prologue

Opening Addresses

Partial Transcript: Keynote Address, Society for the Protection and Reclamation of Indian Images, Seventh Annual Conference, May 3, 1998

Tommy Jack Howkowski

Thank you. Welcome to the Seventh Annual Conference of the Society for the Protection and Reclamation of Indian Images. "SPRY," as we like to call it, is an organization dedicated to the eradication of clichéd and stereotypical images of Indians in whatever mass-market ways they have crept into the national psyche, by exposing these images for what they are, and by then providing positive alternatives. We have, in the recent past, successfully eliminated some of the most degrading sports mascots out there, but, until every last tomahawk has been "chopped," we will continue to be warriors for this cause.

In the year the organization was founded, 1992, the quincentenary of colonialism on Turtle Island, it was important that we consistently sent out the message to mainstream America that we were alive and thriving—that we were, indeed, spry, and now, seven years later, as that celebration fades from the public consciousness, our presence is even more significant.

My name is T. J. Howkowski, and I am this year's conference host. Some of you might recognize me from an appearance on the television show "Justice Scales" last season, in an episode concerning repatriation and adoptions, but only if you didn't blink. Or maybe some of you know me as Professor Howkowski, in the theater department here at the college, and maybe even some of you know me as "Frederick Eagle Cry's son," or, as I am called back home on the reservation, at Tuscarora, where my good friend Dr. Anne Boans also hails from, "Fred Howkowski's boy." Given that bit of history, it is with tremendous pleasure and an overwhelming sense of honor that I introduce tonight's keynote presenter.

Dr. Anne Boans (Tuscarora) was born and raised in the city of Niagara Falls, New York. Her relations had always lived among their people within the borders of the Tuscarora Nation until the introduction of the hydroelectric water reservoir at midcentury, in which the government forced the Tuscarora Nation to sell nearly a third of its precious small amount of tribal land, homes bulldozed and whole families forever displaced under rock and earth and hundreds of thousands of gallons of water, ensuring that much of New York State would have a consistent electrical power source for generations to come. The state needed the reservoir as a backup for peak hours of electricity-generating needs and believed this place was the most appropriate. So, again, indigenous families were removed in the United States' insatiable thirst for power. Dr. Boans's family was among those displaced, living near the border of their ancestral land but not wholly of its national psyche.

Dr. Boans utilized and embraced the unique position this life experience has delivered her and, in true survivor spirit, has developed the keen eye of a cultural observer who is able to see the idiosyncrasies within a group identity and yet be distanced enough from it to offer sharp, pointed, accurate, and often hilarious commentary on the marginalized viewpoints of modern Native America. Armed with several degrees and an impressive presentation list, she has been widely published in many prestigious art history and culture journals, and her monograph on Indian humor in art has recently gone into its second printing. Please join me in welcoming Dr. Anne Boans.

Anne Boans, Ph.D.

Nyah-wheh, thank you, so much for inviting me to deliver the keynote for this year's conference. It is truly an honor, and I will do my best to live up to your expectations. My presentation tonight is called "Threads: The Hair-Ties That Bind." I have prepared a slide show, from my personal collection, of our visual national obsession with stereotypical images of Native America, particularly as manifested in images of braids, as somehow representing the pinnacle of Native identity.

My collection began years ago, when, as a teen, I struggled with the concept of my own identity, attempting to explore where I fit into larger communities, and, admittedly, my initial acquisitions were not made with any sense of cultural juxtaposition at all. I celebrated these images, trying to find my way home in them. In truth, a fair number of these slides did not originate in my own collection but, instead, were borrowed and photographed from the homes of relatives and friends, where the works are displayed with full admiration and embrace and not even the slightest trace of irony.

I have envied some pieces for their succinct capturing of deep cultural confusion and have offered to purchase these outright from the current owners, but in each case my advances have been rebuffed. The owners would no sooner give up these odd icons than they would family members. And, while he is not here, I always publicly thank my husband for aiding me in the procurement of items for my collection. He has the most amazing eye for finding outrageous items that dialogue with this outright exuberant embrace of stereotypes, but I have never dared ask him if he is buying them with culture critique in mind.

As an example, the item in this first slide was a gift from my husband for our seventh anniversary. Here we see a highly traditional bust of a Lakota in war bonnet, mouth wide open, presumably in full war cry, thick braids trailing out from beneath this explosion of feathers surrounding his face. Please note, this item is a bottle opener, the stainless steel lip that catches the bottle cap discreetly embedded behind the resin Lakota man's impressive row of front teeth. So, whenever the person who owns this opens a bottle of beer, the Lakota gets the first drink.

My husband purchased this item at one of the many tax-free cigarette shops that litter most contemporary reservations, where, presumably, a majority of the patrons are going to be peoples of indigenous origin. This in itself speaks volumes about niche marketing and our own communities' involvement in the perpetuation of these stereotypes. In all fairness to my husband the bottle opener was not the only anniversary gift he presented me that year. He also handed me a down payment receipt on a mobile home, which allowed us to move back among our people, where we continue to live, on land that has been his family's since the reservation's inception.

This next slide I have included especially for our esteemed host. I am sure you recognize these plastic Native warrior figures from when you were children, either playing with them or knowing other children who had them and envying them. These were produced in an era in which children's action figures did not come with articulated limbs, and, as a result of the immobility of the figures, they were generally produced in poses suggesting elements of their presumed social standing and class designations. In direct contrast to the other western-themed character figures—the cowboys—who were frequently produced standing surefooted and broad shouldered, hats cocked at jaunty angles as they gracefully slid their revolvers from hip holsters, the Natives were most commonly posed flailing about, limbs stretched far, defying the laws of anatomy and physics. Ever present on these figures, again, thick dual braids mimic the movements of said warrior, frozen in mid-sweep from the warrior's head, two angry vipers, arched and ready for attack.

In this detail from that group of figures we have the local connection I mentioned a few moments ago. While I have found no conclusive evidence that this identification occurred anywhere other than within the borders of our community, it has generally been agreed upon by those of us living here that this figure was based on none other than Fred Howkowski, a.k.a. Frederick Eagle Cry, a.k.a. T.J.'s father. Fred Howkowski had left our community in the 1960s to follow a dream of acting in the movies. I explored his career in depth in my dissertation chapter and subsequent paper, "Silent Screams: The Indian Actor as Angry Landscape in the American Film Western." It is paramount to note that our small local community so embraced these stereotypical images that it chose to identify one of these pieces of molded plastic with its own native son.

The two items in this next slide, while to some degree different, hold at the crux of their metaphors exactly the same idea. What we have here are two collector's plates from the Alexander Mint Company, which seems to specialize in codifying and commodifying images some individual in marketing designates as somehow "truly American" images. From dead celebrities to cherubic flights among the clouds, this company suggests in the global span of their themes that America is in love with that which is unattainable and in some fashion legendary. Falling thoroughly in the pendulum swing between gorgeous foreign dead royalty and handsome yet brusque dead millionaire racecar drivers, we find more of this stereotypical fascination with a particular image of the indigenous peoples of this continent.

On the left we see an image we have seen just a few moments ago, at the beginning of this presentation—the ubiquitous war bonnet–wearing Lakota man standing among the equally ubiquitous buttes and mesas of the American West. And on the right, also in Lakota motif, a young woman, who we might suspect would be referred to as "maiden" in the advertising literature for this particular item, dressed heavily in a beaded buckskin outfit, kneeling subserviently in an overgrown meadow. The metalanguages of these two images, the relationships each figure has with its particular setting, are extremely sexually charged. The mesas surrounding the man are tall and narrow, shooting straight up into the pure sky, clearly strong phallic symbols suggesting the man's virility, while the meadow in which the young woman kneels is flooded with wildflowers, suggesting she is naturally among those wildflowers, open, receptive, and in full blossom herself, begging to be deflowered, as it were.

While these curious parallel elements are deeply disturbing in and of themselves, other, even more alarming suggestions are made by the rest of the compositions. Please observe, in each case, the Native figure seems to have some nearly supernatural relationship with an animal, as if we were all dark-skinned Dr. Dolittles, chatting up our animal friends. Significantly, though, in both cases the relationship is an ominous one, speaking of impending betrayal. The Lakota man holds out his arms, and a bald eagle lights gracefully on the man's wrist, and from what is the man's head accoutrement made primarily? Eagle feathers! Similarly, a spotted fawn rests its head on the young Lakota woman's lap, contentedly nibbling on some wildflower—that would be the young Lakota woman's lap . . . covered in deerskin!

In both cases these individuals are clearly gorgeous and toned, as if, when not cavorting with their animal friends, they are spending much time at Gold's Gym or, in this case, Red's Gym. Are these supernatural gym rats using their unearthly powers merely to cultivate new wardrobe accessories? Again, in both cases, regardless of all other visual dynamics, the one consistent element that tells us explicitly these must be Natives of the Americas—these thick shiny, nearly shellacked-appearing braids—stream from their heads dramatically.

The next slide offers a new twist on the braid motif. I found this in a gallery at the center of town in old Santa Fe, on the plaza, when I was delivering a paper at a conference sponsored by the Art Institute. That it was painted on black velvet, of course, truly set the tone for the piece, but I suspect it would have been as absurd had it been rendered in more traditional fine art techniques and materials.

The painter was selling the work himself, but I did not dare ask him for any further clarification. I feared any dialogue with the artist might ruin what was plainly evident in the piece. The artist called this piece . . . *Jesus and the End of the Calvary Trail*. As we could have guessed from the title, the painter has merged the image of Christ and one of the stations of the Cross with that old western classic, *The End of the Trail*, where the downtrodden Native brave and his nearly broken horse head to the sunset of their lives, engaging these two characters as fellow travelers, a not unoriginal image in its own right, but note! Not only does the dying brave wear braids, but Christ himself has tied down his wavy locks in a herringbone braid as well! One can only speculate that the priest and nuns in the church far off in this painting's landscape must need hair ties as well. The style in which this piece was painted clearly harks back to an earlier era, rejecting the strides made by such contemporaries as Quincy Fisher or Janis SpringBee.

Shirley Mounter 2001

Yes, that's my daughter, shooting off her mouth in public again, though she calls herself Annie out here on the reservation, and she leaves all those other extra letters off, too. Ha! I could get up there and tell things better. I could tell the truth, but they don't usually want to pay so much for that. I was with her in Santa Fe when she bought that piece off that painter, and what she's not saying up there on the stage, with all those other fancy Indians in their coordinated beadwork and fashion ribbon shirts, pretending it's so quaint that someone got fry bread catered for their gathering, is that she saw that painting there, all right, but the rest of the story is a little different. She might say she fell in love with it right then and there, but she still negotiated down, because she said the people in the background weren't clear enough to show what they were. The painter said, "I know what they are," but that wasn't good enough for her, and she made him knock twenty-five off the final price.

But I wouldn't say anything even if they asked me up there on that stage with my daughter. She lets me keep my lies and half-truths, and I let her keep hers. She did until now, anyway. She's a smart one, and I always figured she'd just chosen not to ask me those questions, but I also knew they would come, had even practiced how I might answer them over the years, on occasions when I've been alone.

The answers in my pretend conversations haven't always been the same. Sometimes I said, "No, are you crazy?" Other times, "Yes, and I'm sorry I never told you before." Most often it was something in between, an "It's possible," which you'd think might be an easier answer, but it truly wasn't. It takes into account both possible paths Annie might be looking for and implicates me without giving her any satisfaction. I leaned more toward that one because it seemed to suit the reality of my life.

"Ma!" she said, firm, when I picked up the phone this morning. I was drinking my first morning cup and had worked my way through part of the newspaper. "You busy? I'm coming over in a while. How full is the back bedroom?" she said. Her mother-in-law's TV was on in the background with those overly perky eight in the morning people.

"Odds and ends, as usual, why?" I said.

"I have something I need to talk to you about, so don't leave, okay? See you in a bit." Where was I going to go? I didn't even own a car. I had to rely on my boy, Royal, or anyone else who stopped by to give me rides to the store or wherever, if they were going. I have to do my shopping by the needs of other people's bellies and hope we're hungry at the same time of the week. She hung up, and I went to clear the back bedroom of my things and see what I might do with Royal's stuff, too. I knew, hanging up, that, when she got here, there was likely to be some major shift in her life, and I was going to be the one cleaning up again, putting things back together.

I had already guessed Annie's mother-in-law had more than a hand in this. Martha Boans has never been the easiest to get along with, and we go way back, Martha and me, but my Annie knows the good side of a fight, too. My daughter used to always like the city life, said it toughened her up, but that's not really true. She liked being anonymous, walking down the street, changing her curtains, buying a new car, and not having a couple hundred other people commenting on these things, which is the way it is out here. It took some getting used to, I'd be the first to admit, but I had a head start. I'd spent all my growing up years here and some of my adult life, before the state uprooted us like bad teeth. The nerves inside those teeth supposedly die when they're yanked, but, I can tell you, they throb for a long time, and then they only grow sleepy. Those nerves never die.

I'd known Martha for years, and our shared history was one of complications. So, when my daughter married her son, Dougie, it was just another level. Then, on their anniversary seven years ago, two things happened, and Annie felt the yank, deep, and I swear, she still to this day throbs with it and believes Dougie somehow set up both those things to bring her to this point. The first thing was his gift. The second, who could say why it happened? These stories fold, cross over, split, and reassemble themselves, and, though we'd known each other for years before, the first pulled thread was probably the one where my husband sold my house to Martha's husband on a drunk one night, and we didn't know a thing until after money and paper had exchanged hands.

Border One

Burying Voices

Fred Howkowski

Forgetting. That's what this is really about: trying to sort out those times in your experience with someone that you'd just as soon not have to carry around with you for the rest of your life. They tell you it's about remembering, when they try to sell your family the inspirational cards with your entry and exit dates and some moving verse, the guest book, the thank-you cards with matching envelopes, the obituary with the carefully worded language—in this case, "died suddenly"—the urn, the nameplate, the concrete sealer. That one is a harder sell on the reservation. It's required by law most places but not at home. We don't mind that our dead grow back into the earth, so the man in the black suit and sedate tie tries to apply the laws of physics to my family's grief, not knowing his pitch ensures the exact opposite reaction. He suggests that the back hoe is heavy, and, if the newly turned earth sinks at the wrong time, my urn could crack open under all that pressure, and then I'd be spilling out all over the place. Those white people, they think that's a bad thing, but, once all the people from home get me in place, they know their jobs.

These suspension straps lower me into the hole then slide out from under me, and the last ritual begins. They want to pretend they're helping to bury me, my last mortal remains, but what they really drop down into this deep hole are memories, unwanted, muddy thickly clotted memories, laced with roots and worms and beetles, the occasional termite.

My father is first. I recognize his hand immediately. He lets the dirt fall in hard clumps, hitting the top of my urn. I wonder if he's using two hands to pick up a large enough chunk. He's looking to make a dent, leave a mark, anything. Here we are, when I'm seven, and we get our first TV, and he lets me know, as soon as my mother leaves the room, that I am not to tell my friends we have one, since he doesn't want his house filled up with TV-less Indians, who should be out looking for jobs, anyway, instead of watching his TV, and he even closes the front curtains when he has it on, so no one can see its glow, as if that large metal antenna on the roof didn't give our situation away, and here we are at my eleventh birthday, when he hands me a three-pack of rubbers and tells me to keep these in my wallet at all times because you never know when opportunity is going to knock, and I better not even think about knocking some girl up because we can't afford to feed even one more mouth, let alone two, and here we are, when I let him know I've been drafted and am soon to be a father myself, that it's clear the thing that troubles him more is not that I'll be taking lives and risking my own but that I'll be bringing a new one into the world. Maybe those are enough memories for him to get rid of at this moment. I'm sure he doesn't want to linger inappropriately, so he'll be back later.

My mother is second and even a little unsteady in the way she tosses the dirt in. She sprinkles it like she would powdered sugar on top of fry bread on occasion. She doesn't want to give up that many memories, but I know the ones she's dusting me with. They are those last few weekends I come home on leave, saving all my pay so I can get back here, and she grows more and more busy every time I return. That last time she asks me not to come back, that it's too hard to see me leave, and I can see she'll be relieved when I head out for Vietnam for good, so she can begin the forgetting process in earnest. She's been rehearsing for this minute going on five years.

My little brother, Gary Lou, holds her hand and tosses his own handful in, small clumps of memory, mostly fear. And here we are, me yelling for my gun from my room in the middle of every night, and he remembering mostly that he wishes I never came home, so he wouldn't have to experience this stranger sleeping in the next room, this stranger who's wearing his brother's face. He's holding onto all those other memories, the ones of the brother he knew before. He's not giving a one of them up.

And here's Nadine Waterson, sinking the heels of those fierce "come jig me" shoes she wears on a Saturday night. She kicks some clumps in and grabs one big chunk to toss my way. And here we are when she tells me the boy isn't even likely mine but that I can have him if I want. She's wanting me to be pissed, hurt, anything, and it's her own disappointment that she dumps here, when she realizes that I don't care, as long as he has a chance at a good life. She'll rewrite this one so that I'm the sucker after all, and she's free to do so.

And Martha Boans comes along in her prim dress, not black exactly, gray, maybe it had been black at some point. And here we are, at her table, and she's asking me why I brought that awful man back with me who's been ruining Shirley's reputation. And here we are after I say Shirley's a big girl and can make her own decisions. I guess, if Martha can make that conversation go away, she thinks she can make Tommy Jack himself go away.

And Shirley Mounter finally steps up. She's been circling through this crowd, coming close to the hole, stepping back, moving between people, but finally she chooses a firm clod and breaks it in two. She gives up precious little. She drops in one piece from the clump in her hand and tosses the other back to the mound, as if others won't pick up that piece. And here we are when I tell her on the phone that the little people are following me all around Los Angeles, that they're trying to protect me, the way they have protected lost Indians forever, but that I see them less and less, that even the little people are giving up on me and returning to the reservation to protect more deserving souls—this is what she tosses to me. The piece she throws back to the mound I can't see, but we both know what it is—her silence on the other end of the line during that last telephone conversation, her eternal silence.

And my little boy comes up next, but he doesn't have much to drop, very little to spare. He gives one up, a token, because he already knows rituals are expected of him. He chooses well. And here we are, me walking away in the Lubbock airport terminal and he refusing to wave as I step out that door and into a different life.

And Tommy Jack, he steps up and looks down on me as he had hundreds of times over there, in the jungles. I was always clumsier than him, so, when we shared a foxhole, he made me jump in first, since he could always jump in second and not step on me. He holds the dirt up to his face, breathes deep, knows the scent of earth around me. Over there we rubbed the dirt on each other's faces, trying, always trying, to disappear. He smudges some into his beard and then lets it drop on me and steps back. The only time he wants to give. And here we are, in my apartment in Los Angeles, but I can't see all that well, because I have blown a significant part of my head off and he doesn't want to look, but he does. He identifies me. And here we are.

And others come, dropping careless pieces, dismissing all memories, good and bad, playing fireball, drinking, shooting pool, pickup basketball games, me throwing up at some party, people who will just vaguely remember me in a year and only as a momentary flash after that. And here they are, disposing of me as only they can.

And here I am, home. And here I am. Home.

Border Two

Burning Memories

Really almost nobody sees this happen, but it's one of those reservation times so outrageous that many people will later misremember the event, as if they had seen it firsthand, like the police evicting us from lands that were supposed to be ours forever. Even those who are present only see their own pieces as they unfold and become parts of the larger moment, their own and not theirs exclusively.

Billy Crews

"Stomp on it, man!" my brother shouts, and I do as I'm told. The pedal goes down, and the pistons pound as our car flies across the dried-out swampland, snapping saplings, screeching straight onto the bush line. We practically lift off, splitting through the growth and into the clearing. "Okay! Enough! Let it off!" he shouts, but, when I do, nothing changes. The pedal stays flat to the floor as we cross a dirt basketball court, where a lone ball brushes by us when we knock it. That's when I see our headlights reflected in windows directly before us.

"It's stuck. I thought you fixed this," I shout, the windows getting closer and closer. Suddenly, he's no longer in the seat next to me, and I'm thankful we decided not to put doors on this piece of junk field car until the fall. I jump from my side, and we lie at the court's edge, dust coating us as we watch our skeleton of a car fly straight over to Martha Boans's house. The car—frame, seats, engine, and gas tank—zeros in on her dining room like it was being pulled in on a fishing line.

"Why didn't you aim it somewhere else before you jumped?" my brother says, punching me, knuckles out, so hard that my shoulder's gonna carry bruises for weeks. Then we both see exactly where it's going to connect and scramble up as fast as we can. A second later the car hits.

Floyd Page

My cousin Innis and I are shooting hoops with some skins from down the road, near Martha Boans's place. Innis is related to her on his dad's side, so we have playing rights on their court. She's home tonight, sitting in the window. We wave, and Innis says we might stop over for a glass of iced tea after the game. He hadn't been to see her in a while and said it wouldn't take more than a few minutes. I'm always up for a good glass of tea, so that works for me. We're up nineteen to three when the distant field car we'd heard all evening grows abruptly louder. The car crashes through the woods, and we clear out to someone's back porch until those crazy bastards pass on by. I don't recognize the car at first, and you never want to take chances on an unknown like that. As it rolls out beyond the trees and into view, I see it's a couple of those Crews boys. They're not stopping, and suddenly they're diving out of the car as it flies toward Martha's house. I run for it, but there's nothing I can do. I'm fast, but outrunning cars isn't in my book. It hits the house and keeps going.

Martha Boans

I leave my usual chair in the window where I watch the world go on by. I have just finished sewing the front of a new blouse that I know, once I finish it and put it on, will bring Barry home for good. He won't be able to take his eyes off of me, even after all these years, once I have this on. I hold it up to myself in front of the large three-quarter-length vanity mirror on the wall in here. The fit is perfect. I have every measurement exact. The back is spread out on the dining room table. I should be able to finish it later tonight. I am not much of one for the TV after the quiz shows, but tonight I have an itch that there must be something coming for me across the airwaves, and my fingers are a little sore, so I pick up the remote control and sit on the couch with my sewing. It won't take but a couple of minutes to run through the channels, first the networks and then the Canadian stations, and by then my fingers should be rested enough to continue on my blouse. I press the power button on the remote control, and the world explodes around me.

Every window in the room blows outward, a million diamonds scattered to the wind, and I'm knocked to the floor by some force I never see coming. Heat rolls in over me. The glass from each framed photograph snaps and slides down my walls. My kids in their baby pictures, graduation pictures, wedding pictures, all stare out, suddenly free of the glass that has trapped them forever at those points in their lives. The mirror shows me a glimpse of my dining room and kitchen just before it falls from its frame and sprays me with a thousand small reflections of myself. I cover my head but peek out into the dining room, and what I had thought had to be wrong is indeed confirmed for me there.

A car rocks in the middle of the room, where my old solid cherry table normally sits. My overhead light swings back and forth over it, casting dancing shadows over the whole room. The car is naked of its skin, the sheet metal all cut away and the frame welded together. It's one of the hundreds of field cars on this reservation that wander through its secret woods. This one is different from most others. It's on fire. The car's still running, its wheels spinning into the splinters of my old wood floors. If those treads catch, the car might come further. I'm relieved to see that at least there's no one inside of it. My table is pushed and shattered up against the stairway. My cupboards have fallen onto the engine compartment. Dishes, coffee cups, even those cartoon character jelly glasses, lay all over the car. I guess it has no windshield. I spring out of its way with energy I didn't even know I had and leap toward the front porch.

A second explosion knocks me back into the living room. Two of my propane tanks disappear in a giant burst of flame. The third is still lodged in the hole near the back end of the car, pointing in, like a missile, straight at me, waiting to go off. I run back into the living room. A lifetime of memories sits here: pictures, bowling trophies, the desk that contains all my papers. Blue flashes surround me as wires fray and melt, sending a shower of sparks out into my direction, and then my room goes dark, my electricity gone for good. The flames light my way, and I am left with no choice but to jump from one of my windows and leave everything behind. I cross through the frame in midair as another blast hits me straight on, carrying me through.

Fiction Tunny

I'm putting some finishing beadwork flourishes on new dance outfits when I hear the explosion. Sound doesn't carry all that well through the reservation's dense woods, so it must be close. I step outside and wave to Shirley Mounter, who's driving by and pulling into Mason Rollins's place to fill her car's tank. A small feather of smoke drifts up from mid-reservation. Even the sight brings me back to my own house fire, the things hopelessly lost, the charred pieces of your life that you can hold as they flake away into ash, never to return, no matter how much you might hold them close and wish. I wonder what that person has lost, how this fire will change them.

I go back inside and look through my beadwork to see what I might be able to raffle off to benefit whoever it is, if need be. I look up the Red Cross number for emergency help and then walk over to Mason Rollins's smoke shop to reserve a tentative date for a benefit dinner and raffle, or whatever, in case this fire is not tires or big trash or any other insignificant burning. I can't bring a lot of immediate help here, but what I can bring is the knowledge of loss—maybe even just a hand to hold that knows some of the third-degree burns are not visible to anyone else. It's not a big contribution to make, but it's all I've got.

Shirley Mounter

I pick up some vanilla ice cream and a six pack of Vernor's ginger ale at Mason Rollins's shop after I fill the tank. It's nice that he carries some groceries now and not just cigarettes anymore. I'm in his parking lot when Fiction Tunny calls my name and points to the eastern sky, where smoke is just beginning to rise. I nod, seeing that another fire is the new bad news on our small reservation. I can't help myself from speculating who, this time, will lose out because these chiefs won't allow city fire hydrants within the bounds of our territory. I promise myself to glance up only as I pass by and make note of whose it is. I'll probably begin work tonight on a new quilt for raffling purposes at the benefit dinner that's sure to be, maybe even teach Martha some stitches and get her to help me with one. I'm on my way to visit her, though she doesn't know I'm coming. I'm just dropping in, figuring she'll be alone, with all of our in-town kids together celebrating out somewhere. Tonight we're going to have Boston Coolers to our hearts' delight. We're not so adventurous as our children, but there's no beating a cooler on a warm, early-summer night.

Like most out here, I would tend to follow smoke, but tonight I've got ice cream growing soft in my passenger's seat. Martha and I keep each other company a lot as the years have gotten on and our men have done their vanishing acts. I quit chasing Harris long before now, and she's settled into Barry making occasional guest stints at her place, like it's a reservation Holiday

Inn or maybe detox. I tend to stay away when Barry's around. It's odd enough being in the house that had been mine, on any day seeing the things Martha's put up on my walls, doors Barry's cut into walls for additional rooms, but I've grown used to it over the years, as you do, like rubbing a scar when it aches in the cold. But, anytime I see Barry in that house, I can picture him all over again, with that measuring tape and that shit-eating grin, and it's more than I can bear. I know my limits most times. Martha's come to similar conclusions as far as her husband is concerned, too. If he comes home and decides to stay a bit, she calls me up, packs a bag to come stay with me until he gets the hint, moves back to his old ways, and just wanders on out into the world again, drinking and cursing and wondering where his old life went, like the rest of us.

Bob "The Hack" Hacker

I am on my third lazy off-duty beer in the private volunteer firefighters' bar when a reservation call comes in across the radio. We run to get dressed and rush out the door, but out there it's always a waste of time, our jobs sad and ridiculous. With no city water and sewer lines, when a reservation house catches fire, you better just kiss it good-bye because, by the time we can get there with the water trucks, we're merely doing damage control, keeping the fire contained to one house. I know that reservoir is a major sticking point with them, but they're just crazy, as far as I can tell. We've begged and pleaded with the reservation leadership to let water in or even to let us set up several large water tanks around the reservation, so we can have access to them in case of fires, but they're so protective of what little say they have left in anything. They refuse and walk away every time, telling us they would rather see the entire reservation burn to the ground than allow anymore outside interference in their business. Man, they play for keeps, no matter what. Even my buddy Floyd Page, when I ask him about this hazard, all he says is that I might work with a bunch of Indians but I am obviously not one of them. We get on the truck, and I wait to see which acquaintances of mine have had their life jumbled and shuffled by a careless cigarette or a vengeful fight.

Chief Johnnyboy Martin

I'm coming home from shopping in town when I see smoke in the sky over my Nation. As I reach the Nation's edge, a big tail of darkness grows up into the air, a sight I always hate to see. Everyone out here knows everyone else, and I will certainly know the person whose fire this is. With every house not on fire along my way, my heart grows heavy, not wanting to believe what I will eventually see—the tail grows from the remains of Martha Boans's house, where a flaming car is lodged in the wall closest to the driveway.

I know it isn't true, but, anytime I see the disappearance of anything related to the reservoir's coming, I can't help but be suspicious the Tunny family has something to do with it. Bud Tunny might be a dehorned chief, but he still thinks he controls things around here, and he still has a mighty load of guilt over the land his father lost for us in the reservoir, and this displaced house is one of the last physical reminders. After he burned down the trailer of his illegitimate daughter, Fiction, because she dared to claim him, I have no doubt he would have few qualms about destroying other elements of our shared history. Even if this were his own house, though, he is so furious about the mistakes his father made in letting outside influences inside the Nation that he would still refuse to let city water lines into our bounds. This fire, however, looks like it's our community's other enemy, instead—just the stupidity and carelessness of our next generation. I pull over, walk from my car, and, like all others, watch and wait for this sad event to end.

Innis Natcha

Two of my auntie's propane tanks go up like rockets, shooting straight into the summer night when the car hits. The explosion spreads through the house, and her windows spray her lawn with countless shards. She had been in that window a minute or so before, but I can't see if she's still there. All I see are flames, getting bigger by the second. As I pass those idiot Crews boys sitting dazed on the ground, I resist the urge to throw them straight into the fire. Nearing the blaze, I can't even get close to her door, the heat is so intense. Her last tank is just waiting to go off, and there's no way I'll be able to help her with a bunch of metal stabbing into me from that likely explosion. Maybe I can see her from one of the other windows. I clear the front of the house, where her lawn glints with all those fragments of glass. As I round the corner to the back side, I see her, lying on the ground, holding on to some strip of cloth, blood covering her. She looks up.

"Innis. My blouse back. It's on the table," she says, pointing back to the shattered window frame she'd climbed through, as I lift her to stand.

"Auntie, I can't go in there. The whole place is on fire. Come on, I have to get you away from here," I say, but she doesn't budge, leaning back toward the shattered window she must have climbed from. The bottom shards of the pane and the frame there are covered in blood. I look. Somehow she's lost her shoe and her bare foot is raised an inch or so above the grass. That's where the blood is coming from, dripping from her toes, but I can't figure out how she's gotten it all over herself.

"Please," she says, moving back there, so I just grab her and carry her away, making a broad arc through the front of her lawn, as the last tank goes up. I get her to a lawn chair, and my cousin Floyd has brought a wet towel from the other house. She won't look at us or even at the house, as it disappears quickly in large rolling balls of smoke and flame. She stares at that piece of cloth she had with her on the ground. She won't let it go for anything. We put pressure on the gash and clean her foot of the sticky blood as we wait for the water trucks to come.

Mason Rollins

Fiction comes in and shows me the growing pillar of smoke over on the eastern horizon and suggests we may have to reserve the social hall for whoever's troubles these are going to be. I tell her to work, as she always does, with her boyfriend, as he's the one who takes care of that bleeding heart crap for me. Yeah, I know that sounds harsh. And, before, I might even have followed the smoke to see what I could do, and also to be nosy, but what this means these days, since I've come into some money, is that whoever owns this fire will desperately try to find some connection to me, some reason I should give them money.

These days I have set a firm policy: one hundred dollars donation from the Smoke Rings Disaster Relief Fund for any proven calamity any reservation family experiences and use of the hall for a benefit, if they want—nothing more, nothing less. It saves me a lot of hassle.

ELSIE'S BUSINESS

FRANCES WASHBURN

January, 1969: *Funerals*

January 24, 1970: *Insomnia*

January 27, 1970: *Ceremonies and Arrangements*

January 31, 1970: *Wiping the Tears*

February 1, 1970: *The Kindness of Strangers*

February 3, 1970: *Digging Up the Past*

February 4, 1970: *Going Home*

January, 1969

Funerals

Big events happened next over those three days from Saturday night until Tuesday night, three events that set Jackson reeling. First, of course, was the discovery of Elsie's body, but then on Sunday night John Caulfield showed up at the sheriff's office, stinking from a drunk, not that the latter was unusual, but his hysteria was something he had never displayed before, something different from his belligerent drunken state or his sullen, hungover state.

After the deputy had calmed John down enough to understand what he was saying, the deputy put in a shaky phone call to an exhausted Parker to come back to work, while John sat in the cracked leather side chair, shivering and exuding alcohol from every pore. The deputy left him sitting there, marched back to the cells and kicked out the two Indians, told them just to beat it. They stared at him in disbelief and confusion and then walked out, into the gray cloudy cold. The deputy led John, now calm and passive, back to the cell, slammed it and locked it. After pacing the grimy little office for half an hour, the deputy was about to call the sheriff again when Parker walked in.

"All right, what the hell is going on that you couldn't tell me on the fucking phone?" Parker demanded. "I haven't had more than two hours' sleep out of the last twenty-four, so this better be good."

"Shit, boss, I've got John Caulfield back there in the cells," he motioned with his thumb back down the hall. "He just confessed to the murder of Elsie Roberts."

"What! What! What the hell did he say?"

The deputy's eyes were huge. He never expected anything like this to happen to him. He thought it only happened in big cities and on television programs. His head felt big as a watermelon, and he wasn't sure if it was still the flu hanging on, or this other thing.

"He said he'd been pissed at Elsie for months, mad enough to kill her," the deputy went on. "He said that he got drunk last night, or started yesterday afternoon I guess, he wasn't clear on that. I guess he must have bought his first bottle around ten o'clock in the morning. He said—"

Parker interrupted.

"Well, get to it, what the hell did he say about the killing?"

"He says he doesn't remember doing it, but he knows he did it. He says it must have been him."

"That all? That's not a real confession. What the hell does he mean—" Parker stopped himself. "What the hell am I asking YOU for when you got Caulfield himself back there locked up!"

He turned and strode swiftly down the short hall with the deputy right behind him. He opened the door to the cells, and stopped so suddenly that the deputy crashed into his back.

"Christ."

In the cold breeze stirred by the opening door, John Caulfield swung slowly to and fro, his body suspended by his belt from the overhead pipe that carried water to the deputy's little apartment above the jail.

Parker, so exhausted he felt even his ears must be asleep, ransacked Caulfield's cabin and found nothing. No bloody clothes, no nothing. What in the hell made John so sure he had done it, he wondered. The waitress at The Steak House said John had come in for his usual hangover meal—tea and dry toast—and when he heard about Elsie he let out a cry like a dying animal and ran out without his coat, without paying. From the time, Parker figured that John had went straight to the sheriff's office and told his story to the deputy.

Could've been John, he told himself. But he wasn't completely sure.

Elsie's murder came first, and then John Caulfield's confession and suicide. They say things come in threes, good things and bad things. The third bad thing came on Tuesday around noon when Steve Laveaux walked into the sheriff's office. Parker was back on duty after finally getting in eight hours of sleep in a row, but he didn't feel rested or relieved, and the dark circles beneath his eyes had sunk lower down onto his cheeks, like the bottom half of an archery target with his own black pupils as the bull's eyes.

Laveaux was a big man, fat to tell the truth, and how he stayed that way on the meager diet of government commodities was a mystery. Laveaux himself said it wasn't the amount of food he ate, but the kind. He said Indians were meant to eat buffalo and wild fruits and vegetables, not the heavy starchy diet of government handouts.

He stood nervously, moving from foot to foot in the doorway of the sheriff's office. He was bundled up in layers of clothing that, over his naturally big body, made him look like a blanket-wrapped badger, the flaps on his cap sticking out at right angles like mule ears.

"I got some bad news I got to tell you," Laveaux said solemnly.

Parker thought it couldn't be any worse than the things that had happened over the last few days.

"And that is?" he asked.

"You know," Laveaux said. "That long hill going down into Rosebud town from the north?"

"Yeah."

"Well, it's got those deep ditches on either side, you know, and the road is kind of cut into the hill."

"Yeah, yeah. What about it?"

"People get stuck in there when a big snow storm comes through, or they run off the road and get stuck in those ditches. I live right down there at the bottom of that hill, so in the winter I sometimes get people walking into my place."

"So, who walked into your place on Saturday night? Or was it Sunday morning?"

Laveaux suddenly snatched off his cap, as if he'd just remembered it was on his head. His hair stuck out all over his head.

"Nobody. I walked up there to see how deep the snow was on Sunday. I was thinking it might be easier to get out to town for groceries by going that way. The road going out of Rosebud south had a big drift acrost it. The hill road going north was snowed full, bank to bank. But the wind had been blowing and I saw a shiny blue patch sticking up out of the ditch, and I knew it was somebody's car or something. I went over there and dug down to the driver's side window, and there was a person in there, frozen solid." He stopped there as if he still saw that face, that body frozen bolt upright, hands on the steering wheel, head tilted back a little with the eyes closed and the cheeks slightly rimed with frost like a three day growth of white beard.

"Oh, God," Parker said, pressing his hand to his forehead. "And who might this victim be?"

Laveaux pressed his lips together as if to keep the name inside.

Parker stared at him.

"There wasn't any way to get through up Rosebud Hill. It's gonna take a snowplow or spring thaw to clear that out. Took me and my neighbors all day Sunday and Monday and half of this morning to dig through that snowbank on the road coming south out of Rosebud. I came as soon as I could. It's Donald Marks," Laveaux said.

Parker swallowed hard, thought of Nancy. He knew it was going to be a long time before he got another eight hours of sleep in a row.

Nancy was double numbed, walking through her days in a dream, one part of her mind continuing all the busy work chores that she always did—cooking, cleaning, knitting—but not much knitting, because she had gotten so adept at it that her fingers held the needles and made the stitches of their own accord, leaving her mind too free to think. She got a neighbor boy to help her, and the two of them took on the daily task of feeding the two hundred plus head of pregnant cows, replacement heifers, and herd bulls—Donald's work, but she didn't think of that, wouldn't think of that. It was just physical labor that tired out her thin body and allowed her fall asleep faster at night, when the house was dark and empty as it had been so many times before when Donald had taken off, but this time, not to return. She tried not to dwell on the obvious connection between Elsie and Donald, not the why or the where or the when. She refused to see the face of the mummified baby, but she dreamed, and in her dream the baby was both of her dead sisters, Mary and Margaret combined into one. The baby should have been her own, the one she had at last given up on having and holding, warm, soft, and smelling slightly of milk and baby powder, sleeping gently in her arms.

She hated Donald. She loved Donald. She thought about all the times when he left her alone on his prowling nights, all the times when she worried that he might have been in a car accident or something, about all the times she wished he was dead. And now he truly was dead.

She made the funeral arrangements, went through the embarrassment of the service feeling the waves of pity that came from the people in attendance, felt the genuine sympathy and support of Father Horst, who appeared to need more sympathy than he gave, as if his store of human kindness was close to exhaustion and only his faith kept him on his feet, saying prayers, patting her shoulder.

The coroner's inquest into the death of Elsie Roberts and that of the mummified baby or fetus found at her house was held on Thursday, the day after Donald's frozen body had been brought back to Jackson, propped like some bizarre mannequin on the seat beside the snow plow driver, who had dug Donald's pickup out of the snow with the help of all the Indian neighbors, Coroner Frank Staley, and Sheriff Ed Parker.

The inquest was a public hearing, after all, and every curiosity seeker in town was there, overflowing the room in the courthouse, out into the halls, waiting for information to be whispered down the standing line like that old game called telephone, or gossip. The information that the people on the end of the line got was as garbled as the results in the game, as multiple shocking bits of information came down the line, but the inquest conclusions came out on the front page of the *Jackson Messenger* on Friday: death at the hands of person or persons unknown for Elsie, and for the fetus or baby, which could not be exactly determined, death by unknown causes. That decision on Elsie's death had been pushed through by Sheriff Parker, in spite of John Caulfield's confession. The deputy testified that John was in a bad emotional state, and he had only said he *must* have done it. Besides, John was a crazy drunk, who might say anything, had a belligerent attitude, but he had never ever really hurt anyone. He might have just snapped and killed her, Parker testified, but personally, he didn't believe it.

If Elsie's murder shocked the town and gave them a titillating topic of conversation, the revelation about the mummified baby found under her bed sent them into an ecstatic state of hyper gossip. Of course, everyone assumed that the baby had been the result of the rape back in Mobridge, but Frank Staley's testimony at the inquest threw doubt on that idea, and then the gossip went to an even higher level.

Staley testified that he couldn't pinpoint time of death or the age of the mummy, but that it was *at least* a year old. Dr. Weston from Mobridge, who had cared for Elsie after the rape, was embarrassed. He admitted that he had not given Elsie a pregnancy test after the rape, as he should have done, he said, but now he couldn't say whether or not she had become pregnant as a result of the rapes; however, he thought that with all the trauma she had endured it was unlikely that she had become pregnant. His testimony was discounted by the local physician in Jackson, Dr. Horgan, who testified that in his own practice, he had treated women who had become pregnant as a result of violent rape. And Dr. Horgan dropped yet another tantalizing piece of information: Elsie had recently given birth, within the last six weeks, but no one had turned up a second fetus. Had it been only an early term fetus, naturally aborted? A full term baby dead at birth, or worse yet, murdered by Elsie? If the second baby had been a full term birth, where was the child? Nothing had turned up in a further search of Elsie's cottage.

Neither Sheriff Ed Parker, nor Dr. Horgan, nor any of the other witnesses had answers to those questions. That very absence fueled the rumor mill. The second child was buried somewhere on the property, and would turn up with spring thaw. The second child has been given to one of the women in the Indian community, and everyone eyed the newborns in town speculatively. The mothers took to leaving their children at home. There was even speculation that Elsie had killed the child in some bizarre rite and consumed the body.

On Friday, the coroner released Elsie's body to the county for burial. The funeral was on Saturday, and was as well attended as the inquest had been. Parker stood in the back, in his gray dress uniform, Stetson in hand, and watched the crowd carefully. No one acted suspiciously; there were no dramatic outbursts of emotion, no hymns sung, no shouted confessions, only the dry words of the standard service read out by Frank Staley, coroner and undertaker. Elsie was not a Catholic, not even a Christian to anyone's knowledge, and so Father Horst could not bury her from the church. He felt very badly about that, as he sat in one of the brown metal folding chairs in the front row close to the cheap coffin purchased by the county. But he could have masses said for her soul, and he would do that.

When the service was over, everyone filed by the coffin to stare at Elsie one more time, to comment later about what a good job Staley had done on making her crushed skull look as normal as possible, about the two turtles, one red and one yellow placed on either side of her head, as if they had just crawled up on the white satin pillow out of some dark pool of water.

Nancy attended. It was not a hard decision for her, even knowing what might have happened between Donald and Elsie. Nancy saw Elsie as a victim, a wounded young woman, a child really, who had never recovered from that first situation at Mobridge, who had been drawn slowly and inexorably to this moment. No, she did not blame Elsie, she blamed Donald, and she was terribly afraid of what Donald might have done. She did not so much feel the need to pay her respects to Elsie, as to put in an appearance before the people of the town. They didn't know about the moccasins under Elsie's bed yet, but they would soon, and they would talk. Inevitably, with Caulfield's guilt in question, Donald's would come up next. Nancy wanted to listen at the funeral for any talk that might already be starting, but she heard none, not about Donald anyway.

Nancy recalled the day of Elsie's murder when Donald had fed the cattle around ten o'clock in the morning as he usually did, then went to the barn as he usually did during the winters, when he had the time to repair any machinery that he hadn't had time to do more than patch together during the busy summer season. He came in and ate a late lunch, took a short nap, and around three o'clock said that he was going to town for some machinery parts and to play a few rounds of cribbage down in the Legion Club.

Nancy had reminded him of the weather service warning about a storm coming in, but Donald said he'd probably be back long before it hit, and if it got bad, he'd just stay in town the night. Nancy doubted it all, expected there was a woman somewhere that he was going to see, but she let him have his lie, as usual.

Then Parker had told her that he had found out from his inquiries that Donald had left the Legion Club around nine-thirty or so on Saturday night and hadn't been seen in town after that. Why would he do that, why would he head out across the rez with a storm coming in? Parker didn't have to spell out the possibilities to her. And Donald's truck had slid off into the ditch going north, *up* the hill and away from Jackson. Where had he been going and why? He had been born in this winter hard country, and he knew not to take off across country with a storm coming in. What was he running from? She told herself that maybe he wasn't, maybe there was some woman he was going to see up there north of Rosebud, maybe down in Ghost Hawk Canyon just beyond. That woman certainly wouldn't be coming forward with any information.

Nancy expected there would be gossip about what Donald was doing on Rosebud hill heading away from Jackson in the middle of a storm, but she hoped people would assume it had to do with Donald's philandering, and nothing to do with Elsie's murder. She hoped, not that she cared what people would think of Donald. He was too dead to care about it, and hadn't much minded his reputation when he was alive, but she didn't want to face the whispers behind her back about her husband. But she had loved him. Yes, she believed that. And she had loved Elsie too, and she wanted to keep their deaths separated in her own mind as long as she could.

She was spared an inquest into Donald's death thanks to Staley and Parker, who justified it by saying that someone froze to death under similar circumstances every winter, that this was just another of those tragic events. Let the town speculate all they wanted to later about whether or not Donald should be considered a suspect in Elsie's murder.

The town seemed to believe Caulfield was guilty. He had confessed, hadn't he, even though it was an odd confession. Some certainly considered Donald as an alternative suspect later on, but John Caulfield or Donald Marks, either one was a more comfortable suspect than the third alternative: that some murderer still walked in their midst. The white folks told themselves that if it wasn't Marks or Caulfield then it had to be an Indian affair, that it had to be some conflict or some problem within the Indian community that they knew nothing about, didn't want to know about, except they were afraid that some evil might cross that line from the dark side of town, the Indian side, and attack their own security, their own white lives.

The Indians kept their mouths shut, even among themselves mostly. They worried about Georgie and Porky Pine, whose whereabouts at the time of Elsie's murder couldn't be pinned down exactly. And the others, the men who had seen the deer woman—well, there could be one that they hadn't known about, whose craziness had been hidden. But they didn't really believe that one of their own had killed Elsie. They remembered the deer woman stories, remembered that in the stories, none of the men afflicted had ever attacked the deer woman herself head on. She was too powerful, but they were afraid it *might* have been one of their own, that some new story with a far different twist had come into being in Jackson, and they feared that the end had not been told yet. Elsie was dead, but the Indian community feared the spirit of Elsie as much as they feared her murderer. They smudged their houses with cedar and sage to repel bad spirits.

Then the final funeral was held, the one for Donald, who had not been in a state of grace, but was a Catholic and buried from the church with all the ceremony and dignity that Father Horst could muster under the circumstances. But, like many winter funerals in Jackson, the curtain did not descend on the final act for a few days longer. The ground was too frozen for the actual burial, so the bodies were stored in the morgue at the undertaking parlor for another week. When the weather broke, five final interment services and burials were performed on the same day, one right after the other, before another hard freeze would mean further delay. Frank Staley presided over the burials of Elsie Roberts, John Caulfield, and the mummified baby; then Donald's final interment presided over by Father Horst, and last of all, the burial for an old man who had died of a heart attack was conducted by the rector of St. Mary's Episcopal Church.

Father Horst decided in late February that he should leave the entire premises in an clean and orderly condition for his successor, so when he had done cleaning the rectory, he went out to Elsie's former cottage and started cleaning there. He imagined he smelled decay inside, but of course, it was only his imagination, he told himself, and indeed, he found no more bodies, but he found something else that had fallen down behind the drawers of the bureau. He found Elsie's birth certificate, and when he had read it carefully, he took it over to Sheriff Parker's office. Phone calls were made.

January 24, 1970

Insomnia

It's four o'clock in the morning; your head is buzzing from too little sleep and too much coffee, but now, you think you might have most of the story. Lowan, who had been sleeping on the floor beneath the table, has long since given up and gone to a night nest on the sofa.

"So that's where it got left, huh? Before I came up here, I mean," you say.

Oscar looks as bright as if he's just slept for hours. Must be all those naps he takes during the day, you think.

"Pretty much," Oscar says. "Elsie's story kind of quieted down. Other stories happened. Lots more goes on in small towns than you'd think."

You don't say so, but you know that's true, coming from a small town yourself.

Oscar rubs his chin.

"Let's see. That spring there was that smart ass Blaeger kid drinking and driving in the middle of the day, hit a carload of Indian women and kids broadside. Tore their car right in two and killed about half of them. He got up on manslaughter charges, but it was dropped 'cause he agreed to go in the Army. Stirred up of us Indi'ns from Standing Rock to Pine Ridge to Rosebud, cause an Indi'n doing the same to a carload of white women and kids—well." He just shakes his head. "Course, it ain't over yet, what with Viet Nam and all. The spirits take care of justice, you know. Then harvest season one of the farmers cutting his own wheat got his arm ran into the guts of the combine. Probably would have made it out of that okay if the hired man had of just shut off the thing or reversed the traction gears, but instead he got panicked and tried to pull his boss out. They both got sucked in, and came out in the grain bin all minced up like sausage and those cracked beef bones like I buy for Lowan. The wife came out to see why they hadn't come in to dinner. She ended up in a hospital her own self. Let's see, what happened to her? Oh, yeah, I think she sold up the place and moved to some family of hers in—where was it? I think it might have been California."

He's quiet for a minute, and you hope he isn't thinking of any more minced-up farmer stories to tell you.

"Course," he says, "there's always the usual number of pregnant teenagers having to drop out of high school and get married. One of them was Ed Parker's oldest daughter. Like to broke his heart and tore up his own marriage, 'cause he blamed himself, and his wife blamed him for not being home more." He pauses. "You know, I've been thinking. There just ain't enough entertainment for kids around here," he says. "Not enough toys, either. They end up with nothing to play with but themselves."

He slaps the table and announces that it's time for bed.

You hear the sounds of tooth brushing in the bathroom, spitting in the cracked porcelain sink, the toilet flushing, and when he comes out, Lowan jumps up off the sofa and follows into Oscar's little bedroom behind the living room.

You lie in the bed in your own room, surrounded by the dark rounded shapes of Mrs. Oscar's clothes piled on the floor, comforting in their presence. Your eyes are permanently opened by the stories and the coffee, and you wonder if you can ever sleep again. Oscar was right. Elsie's story was too big to be told all at once. This last chunk has almost done you in.

You spend the next few days just lounging around the house with Oscar and Lowan, mostly, except for a couple of trips uptown to the grocery store. You buy some food to contribute to Oscar's menu—bacon, eggs, dried pinto beans instead of the navy beans that Oscar usually cooks, hamburger, bread, milk, and fruit—apples that you picked out while avoiding looking at the pyramid of oranges right next. You'd like to cook some ribs for Oscar with some Texas hot barbecue sauce, but to do it right you need a barbecue pit where they can be smoked. Oscar doesn't own such a thing. Ribs aren't right if they are cooked in an oven. At the checkout counter you remember you were going to buy some grits, and you ask the clerk for the whereabouts, but the aisle she sends you to is lined with canned goods, and when you ask the clerk idly flicking the cans with a green feather duster, he points at the cans of hominy. You give up, pay for what you got, and go back to Oscar's house.

In between watching Oscar's game shows, you ask a few more questions.

"Where you figure that mummy baby came from?" you ask.

Oscar shakes his head.

"Don't know. Could be Elsie's, but could be something she carried down here from Mobridge. She did get to collect some things of her mother's house that she brought with her. Could've been Mary's baby. Elsie's little sister or brother."

"You think?"

"Naa. I think it was Elsie's. I think she had it that first winter after she came down here."

"Think she aborted it?"

"Naa. If she was going to do that, why wait until it was full term? Frank Staley said it could have been a full term baby, just small 'cause it had been dried up like that."

"The second baby. The one she had just before she died. Is there more to that story? They ever find it?"

"Never did. Tore up the ground all around that house, too. There wasn't so much as mouse bones buried. Plenty of mouse shit, though." His shoulders shake.

You wonder about that. You wonder if there is a child growing up somewhere around Jackson that will have Elsie's full lips, long legs, and healthy musculature, a boy maybe, whose Elsie-inherited features might not be noticed or remarked upon. But what about the father's features?

"What did Donald look like?" you ask.

Oscar looks at you speculatively.

"Blond. Big blond guy, burned red as a beet in the summer. His mother was a Swede. And before you ask, Caulfield was just a plain old white guy—nice looking, but just regular. You know regular brown hair, regular eyes. Just regular."

"Seems to me he was pretty irregular for a regular guy," you say.

Oscar's shoulders shake again.

January 27, 1970

Ceremonies and Arrangements

You're back at Coroner Staley's office again, but this time the redheaded secretary is already there, digging through papers on the desk top, again. You wonder if that's her official job designation: digger. Or maybe desk diver. She barely glances up at you.

"He's not here," she says unnecessarily.

"Well, ma'am, will he be in today?"

"Doubt it. Had a couple of deaths over the weekend." She finishes rifling one stack of papers, shuffles them back together, starts on another.

"Anyone I know?"

She doesn't get your humor.

"A stillborn baby and old man Seivers. The old man died in his house with the heat on high, and the neighbors didn't find him for two days. It's a hurry-up deal."

Halfway through the second stack of papers, she finds a yellow form, pulls it out with an "aha!"

"Now, what can I do for you?" she asks.

"Never mind," you say.

You walk half a block up the street, jaywalk across to Staley's funeral parlor, and you don't even wonder if one of the few cars and trucks parked on the street belongs to Jack Mason. Or you wonder only a little. When a threat is constant, after a while, you get used to it, kinda. You think about it, but you just can't live in a constant state of high alert, but your blood pressure probably stays higher than it ought to be. Maybe the man doesn't really exist, you think, because everybody talks about him, but he never seems to put in a personal appearance to you. He's the bogey man in the dark.

The funeral parlor is by far the best decorated place in town, with thick carpets, pale green painted walls hung with tastefully blurry landscape paintings and a lighted picture of Jesus. A gray sofa and pair of chairs sit against the far wall with a Bible on an end table. There's an announcement board on an easel that lists upcoming funerals, a couple of memorial books to sign on a tall table, and off to one side, a mahogany desk in an alcove. A corridor leads off the reception area to the viewing rooms. Staley's wife, you assume she's his wife, comes out of the back somewhere, a chunky woman with graying hair wearing a tasteful navy blue suit and dark pumps.

"Hello," she says, "Frank has been wanting a word with you. He's indisposed at the moment, but can you wait for a half hour or so?"

Staley wants to see you? This is ominous, you think. You thank his wife when she brings you a cup of coffee from someplace in the back, fresh brewed and hot. You sip it and you think that Oscar's mud has spoiled you for the taste of good coffee.

Staley comes up the corridor from the back in his shirt sleeves, hurrying. He greets you and invites you to follow him to his office just off the main corridor, where you perch on the edge of a chair, a comfortable overstuffed chair, with two boxes of tissues on the table beside it, and brochures of coffins.

"Sorry, I haven't been available much lately," he says. "I'm the only undertaker in the county so my time isn't really my own."

Even from six feet away across the desk you can smell him, not the smell of embalming chemicals, but the smell of whiskey on his breath. Probably needs it with his kind of life. He probably knows personally almost everyone he has to embalm and bury. Must get to a guy after a while.

"I understand," you say. "You've got your priorities."

"That's right, that's right. But we need to talk about this exhumation. Everyone concerned has agreed to it, I mean, the sheriff and all officials of the county including me. Of course, you understand the weather delay." He stops there, looking intently at you, and you know there is something more here, some other reason for the delay.

"There are laws that have to be followed, you understand."

You nod your head. You suspect you know where this conversation is leading—right around to the wallet in your back pocket.

"I have to obey the laws. I can't afford to get my license suspended, and it isn't just my livelihood, it's that I owe a duty to the people of this county. There aren't many people willing to practice this far out in the middle of nowhere. If I'm gone there isn't anyone willing to take my place."

You see the gold signet ring on his pinkie finger, the pricey furniture in his office, and you have your doubts about what he says. People will live most anywhere if the money is there. Plainly, Staley isn't starving to death. You suppress a sick grin because you've just had a thought. Who undertakes a dead undertaker?

"The exhumation order is approved," Staley is saying, "but there are laws about transporting bodies, especially across state lines. Then some states have their own laws and they're all a little different, but generally, it's this. The body has to be embalmed and enclosed in a coffin that is of a certain minimum standard quality, and it has to be sealed for transport. The original intent is to preserve public health, of course."

It is going to be about money, just like you thought.

"Now, the coffin that Elsie was buried in wasn't the best we have to offer. Not that we didn't do right by the young woman," he hastens to add. "But this county doesn't have a lot of money. The deceased has been buried for just about a year now, so that coffin has bound to have deteriorated to some extent, which means it can't be sealed properly for transport."

"It's my understanding," you say, "that the coffin doesn't go directly into the ground. That the coffin is placed in a vault sort of thing. Like a box to hold the box."

Staley tilts his chair back and steeples his fingers over his chest.

"That's true," he says, "but there are several quality levels of vaults, just like there are coffins, and like I said before, the county isn't rich. So the vault for Elsie Roberts is only guaranteed waterproof for one year."

You wonder how anyone would know if the vault failed before the year was up. It's not like a family would dig up a deceased loved one to check on the deterioration—or nondeterioration—of the vault. But you ask the question that is the only one that matters now.

"How much?"

He tilts his chair forward, opens a drawer and pulls out a form with handwritten figures on it, slides it across the desk to you.

You run down the list of charges for a new vault, new coffin, mileage fees to transport the body, extra money for the driver—down to the triple underlined figure at the bottom. You're glad you're sitting on your wallet in your back pants pocket. You feel the magnetic pull of the paper form, tugging those dollars right out of your wallet and beckoning them into Staley's hand with that gold signet ring, see his fingers closing around them and the bills crumpling in the middle like a fat green paper bow tie. The figure is four hundred dollars more than you have.

You push the paper back across the desk to him.

"Any chance of the city or county helping out on this?"

Staley assumes a sad expression, the one you imagine he wears for every funeral he conducts. He shakes his head slowly.

"No, sorry. The county fund is bone dry. We've already had to bury more indigents than we could afford, mostly Indians. Been a bad flu season up here."

You stand up and put your hat on.

"I'll have to get back to you," you say.

"Well, you do that. I'm sure that if you try, you'll come to the right decision," he says and offers his hand.

You shake hands, as briefly as you can make it.

You walk back to Oscar's house, going through the list of your relatives in your head, but none of them have a penny to spare. You think of your own little piece of property and how many years you struggled to pay it off before you retired, and know that you couldn't pay even the smallest mortgage payment out of your little retirement check. It's not just four hundred dollars that you need. There's also the money to pay for getting yourself back home. You're thinking that maybe you spent your savings on a wild goose chase, all because you had some idea that common decency mattered. It does, but most poor people can't afford it.

When you get back to Oscar's, Irene is there, and you guess that today the boys are in school. You hear Oscar and Irene in excited conversation as you approach the front door, your boots crunching on the frozen snow, but they stop abruptly when you walk in. They can tell by your face that everything has gone wrong.

"What?" Oscar growls. Lowan senses the tense mood and barks out the door as you close it, as if to keep at bay whatever evil spirits have followed you. You sink yourself down on the sofa, tired of it all, tired to the bone, but you tell. You expect an outburst of anger from them, but it doesn't come. Irene and Oscar still sit in their same positions; they just aren't smiling anymore. You know how it is. You've been here before, not in Jackson, but in bad situations, and you know the old saying about the golden rule, that the man with the gold makes the rules.

"Ho eyes," Oscar says. "Long time ago, the government divided up our land and gave pieces of it out to the people, because there were few of us. The *wasicu* knew if they made the pieces they gave out to us small enough, there would be lots of big pieces

left over for them. They gave those old Indians deeds to it, you know, my ancestors, too, but sometimes there were disputes over the best pieces."

You're not in any mood for another one of Oscar's stories, especially not one that starts out with what sounds like it's going to be a boring history, but Irene catches your eye and wiggles her fingers and wrist at you, motioning you to be still and listen. So, you do.

"There was this one man named Two Boys because he was a twin and the other one died. Anyway, he didn't have no family or nothing, but he had been kind of raised by this other Indi'n family, so he wanted his piece of land near their place, but someone else, some *takasi* of the wife wanted that land, too, so the old man gave up his claim and let the wife's cousin have it. He accepted another piece of land quite a ways from them, but he didn't want to live on it. He lived up there around Red Shirt Table with this other one family. So, turns out, the piece of land he got was down near here, and it turned out to be good farmland, flat you know, good dirt. Somehow the *wasicun* overlooked it, and Two Boys got this piece. So then, different *wasicun* tried to get him drunk, you know, get him to sell it, but Two Boys didn't drink. Not much anyway, not enough to lose his sense. So, finally they gave up, and Two Boys leased it to a *wasicu* farmer down here. Every year he had to come to town to get the lease renewed. Him and this farmer would meet up at The Steak House and the farmer would try to get the lease for less money, but Two Boys never gave in. It was good land, you know, make seventy-five bushels of wheat to the acre, for real, not just some farmer bragging. Some years Two Boys could make that farmer pay a little more for that lease, but he always let that *wasicu* think he got the better of the deal. Two Boys played dumb Indi'n, you know. He wore his hair old style in braids, kept the blanket, pretended not to speak much English.

"So this one time, Two Boys comes to town to get his lease signed again and collect his money from the *wasicu*. Well, the guy thinks he's going to intimidate Two Boys, make him feel stupid and little, see, so he brings a bunch of his white friends with him, and they're sitting there around a table drinking coffee when Two Boys comes along. This *wasicu,* he says to Two Boys, *'Hau, kola,'* just like they're old friends.

"Then the *wasicu,* he picks up his water glass and drinks it all, and he says to Two Boys, 'Go get me a glass of water.'

"Two Boys takes the glass and disappears to the back of the restaurant. Comes back with a glass of water. The *wasicu* drinks it and says to Two Boys, 'I'm still thirsty. Get me another glass of water.' Two Boys takes the glass and goes off again.

"All this guy's friends, they're laughing, cause they think it's funny to see this ignorant old Indi'n jump to wait on their friend.

"Two Boys comes back with a second glass of water, and the *wasicu* farmer says, 'I'm still thirsty. More water.' Two Boys takes the glass and disappears again to the back of the restaurant, but he comes back holding the empty glass."

Irene has already started to laugh, so you know she's heard this story before, probably dozens of times.

"The *wasicu* farmer says, 'Where's my water? I'm still thirsty!'

"Two Boys says, 'Can't get you more water. There's another *wasicu* sitting on the well.'

"So, after that they changed Two Boys name. After that they called him Makes Water."

Irene is busting up now, tears running down her face, and Oscar sits there, solemn as if he were in church, shoulders not moving an inch.

You can't help it, you smile, and then you start to laugh, too. And then you spoil it all. You ask, "Well, did he get more money on his lease?"

Irene slaps her forehead, and Oscar just looks at you.

"If I couldn't tell better by looking at you, I'd say you're part *wasicu* yourself," he says.

"You got to *listen* to the stories," Irene says. "They'll give you the answers."

"What answers?" you ask, and you feel like a dumb little kid for asking.

"The answers to everything," she says.

"I got my answer from Staley," you say. "I've done what I can, and it wasn't enough. I thank you for your hospitality, but I have to go home tomorrow. You know anyone can take me to the bus station?"

Oscar shifts in his orange chair.

"Listen," he says. "The Roberts family are going to hold a ghost feast, a wiping of the tears ceremony for Elsie up in the canyon. It's been just a little over a year since she died, so it's time to put away mourning now and let her go from us. We should have done it back in December, but you know, people kind of wanted to forget about Elsie. Until you showed up. You need to go. Kind of put her to rest for you."

"I don't understand," you say. "I thought she wasn't part of—you know—part of everybody else. The Roberts, I mean. Or any of the rest of you folks."

"Well, she wasn't really, but she was everybody's relative, you know. Besides, some of the people are kind of thinking that if they do this ceremony, there won't be any more young men seeing the deer woman. So it's kind of double useful."

"That's what I come here to tell both of you," Irene says. "It's going to be Saturday. At some cousins of the Roberts' up in Ghost Hawk Canyon. My husband and I will come get you both early Saturday morning."

January 31, 1970

Wiping the Tears

The sun isn't up yet on Saturday when Oscar calls you for coffee and breakfast. While you're eating as few of his pancakes as good manners will allow, you ask him if there is anything you should know about this ghost feast ceremony, anything that will be expected of you.

"Just stick beside me," he says. "I'll tell you what to do when."

You're still nervous when Irene and her husband, Roger, and the boys show up. Roger is a big man, his bulk filling half the front seat, his head almost touching the head liner of the car. He gives you a quiet greeting. You and Oscar get in the backseat and the boys curl up under blankets and go back to sleep as you make the drive west out of Jackson, up the long hill past the tourist cabins where John Caulfield used to live in Number 8A. The car is filled with the smell of cooked meat coming from a lidded big pan on the floor between Irene's feet so it won't tip over.

You look at Oscar, and he explains, "For the feast," points his lips at a bag of groceries on the floor of the back seat. A can of coffee is on top.

A few miles west of town, Roger turns off the highway onto a narrower paved road to a little town he tells you is Greasy Water. There's a little store and a gas station there, a few houses scattered nearby, but soon the pavement ends and Roger drives slowly through tracks worn into the snow, over roads that wind here and there like a line of string carelessly flung out on the ground.

The sun is full up when the car suddenly drops down a steep hill into a canyon in the prairie, totally unexpected from the flat perspective, until you are there and going down through a one lane cut in the snow. The hill is so steep that your ears pop, and at the bottom the road widens a bit, the tail end of the car slithers on a slick spot.

The boys, wide awake now, yell, "Do it again, Dad, do it again!"

Through the pines and winter bare cottonwoods, you glimpse a frozen creek yards off the road, and you think of catfish jumping in hot summer weather, cut up catfish dipped in cornmeal batter, frying up golden brown in big black skillets.

A couple of miles farther on, Roger turns the car sharply to the left between berry thickets onto a road that you wouldn't even have noticed was there except someone has shoveled a way through the snow for cars. Back into the thickets and the trees sits a log house, small, with smoke rising from a tin chimney, and in the yard, half a dozen cars and men standing around several fires that have been lit in a circle. There's a big shed with double doors opened and a table inside with stuff piled on it.

"That's for the giveaway," Oscar says, and then seeing you don't understand, he says, "It's customary. Most ceremonies include a giveaway from whoever is sponsoring it. The Roberts this time, except since this wasn't really planned far enough in advance, so other people have contributed stuff."

You look at the goods piled up and see there are cases of soda pop, a couple of blankets, cans of coffee, bags of sugar, other stuff, too. Somebody better take that soda inside pretty quick, you think, before it freezes and busts the cans.

Roger stops the car and everyone gets out, the boys yelling and rushing towards half a dozen other kids piling out of the cabin. Irene carefully carries the big pan of meat in front of her into the house.

"Hau, kola," Roger hollers at the men. One of them comes over to him and they clasp shoulders.

"Ho eyes, tokeske oyaunyanpi huo?" the man says.

"Hena, waste yelo."

You and Oscar are looking over the selection of goods.

"Who's it for?" you ask.

"Everyone," he says. "Everyone takes something. Doesn't look like much yet. There'll be a lot more by tonight."

By tonight. Looks like a pretty big pile already to you. You look at the small cabin, at the cars and people already here and know that they won't all fit into that house. It's going to get damned cold before this is over, you think, understanding now the reason for those bonfires in the yard.

The cars and the trucks keep coming, the giveaway pile grows, and you and Oscar are asked to help others build what looks to you like an igloo made of bent-over tree limbs with the ends secured in the middle. It's a small structure, with a hole dug out in the middle, and when you're done, some tarps are thrown over it, the edges weighted down with rocks.

"What's this for?" you whisper to Oscar.

He grunts as one of the tree limbs comes undone, whips back, and slaps him in the gut.

"Sweat lodge," he says.

"What's that?"

"To sweat, what else?" Then he explains more. "It's a purification rite for the *wicasa wakan* before he performs the ghost ceremony."

The *wicasa wakan,* as Oscar points him out to you, doesn't look like anybody special, just an old man, older-looking than Oscar even, with a red wool scarf tied on his head under a battered cowboy hat, and layers of clothes covering his skinny body.

Late in the afternoon, as if a silent gong had rang that everyone except you had heard, women pour out of the little house like columns of ants, the men gather and the crowd becomes silent. The *wicasa wakan* steps out of the sweat lodge, his body, naked from the waist up glistening with sweat, reflecting the dying sun and the red flames of the bonfires. A big drum sits in the middle of the crowd on top of an upended old car hood, put there, you suppose, to keep the bottom of the drum dry. Five men crouch around it, each with a single drumstick. They strike the drum in unison, the sound continuing and echoing and behind you in the crowd a voice begins to sing. The *wicasa wakan* takes up his redstone pipe.

Some children are scuffling in the back and one of the women says to them, "Shhh, *anagoptanye! Wastepe!*"

It begins.

Twenty-eight years you swept the floors, mopped them, waxed them, buffed them. You picked up the pieces of broken chalk from the classrooms, you scrubbed out the toilets and unclogged them when the kids dropped stuff down there that shouldn't be dropped down there. You knew that Mrs. Clayton in fourth grade room 27 was a stickler for having the blackboards washed every week, that Miss Ingersol in second grade room 11 didn't much care about the blackboards, but her trash cans, by God, better be emptied every day. You learned about that look on Principal Adams's face, that look that meant you better stay down in the basement repairing broken desks or anywhere out of his way. You watched kids come into kindergarten and go up the scale of grades and out the other side, and some of them you remembered because they were good kids and some of them you remembered because they weren't. You looked forward to the summers when you could stay home and tend your garden and go fishing. You accepted the summers when you had to find some other work to make ends meet, the summers when you had to go places you didn't want to go and never wanted to see again.

And then the last years came, when your knees hurt so from arthritis that it was hard to bend them, when the floor polisher kick as it hit spots with too much wax made your spine feel like a whip being cracked, and you loaded up on pain pills to sleep at night, so you could get up in the morning and do it all over again. The last graduation. The speeches and congratulations and thank yous and the piddly retirement pay that was all right because you'd saved your money for years. Money that you'd mostly spent now for Elsie. The gold watch on your arm, the traditional retirement gift that you didn't think would mean a stinking thing to you but did.

The ceremony is ended. The people are lining up for the giveaway. Oscar pushes you into line, and you move forward shuffling in the snow. The woman ahead of you says to her companion something about that red blanket on the end and she hopes it's still there when it's her turn. The line moves forward, pauses, moves forward, and the pile dwindles some and it's your turn, but you stand there and wonder what on earth you would do with any of this stuff. You could always use the groceries, but it feels silly to carry it back on the bus.

Oscar nudges you.

"Take something," he says.

You step forward. You reach up your coat sleeve, pull off your gold watch, and place it carefully on top of a ten pound bag of sugar. Step away. For Elsie.

When the gifts are all gone, the women bring out the food from the house and put it on the emptied table where all the giveaway stuff had been. The people line up again, filling their plates, standing or squatting around the bonfires and eating. They go back for seconds, and then they bring out their *wateca* buckets to fill up with the leftovers. As the women are cleaning up the tables, the drums begin again. You're tired and exhausted and cold, and you can't believe there is more to this ghost ceremony.

The *wicasa wakan* spreads a blanket on the cleanest patch of snow he can find and begins to speak in Lakota. The people line up yet a third time, dance in a slow dipping, one-two rhythm past the spread blanket dropping coins and bills as they pass. There are at least a hundred people, and the dance is slow. When it is done the drums give a final thump. The *wicasa wakan* gathers the corners of the blanket together bagging the money in the middle, walks through the snow and hands it to you. Your arms are frozen at your sides.

The *wicasa wakan* bounces the blanket up and down, making it jingle and rustle. Oscar nudges you so hard you almost fall over.

"Take it," he says.

You take the blanket and the *wicasa wakan* steps back.

"Say 'thank you,'" Oscar whispers, but the heavy blanket has weighted your tongue.

"Pilamaya," he says for you, turns and shouts to the crowd, *"Pilamaya!"*

There are nods of assent, smiles, here and there a muttered *waste yelo, waste k'sto*. The people head towards the cars carrying their *wateca* buckets and tired kids.

Waste yelo.

February 1, 1970

The Kindness of Strangers

The money is spread out on Oscar's table in neat stacks of change and paper bills—quarters, nickels, dimes, a few tens, one twenty, and a whole lot of ones. You've counted it three times, and it keeps coming up the same. $316.25. Oscar reaches for the Big Chief tablet and the stubby yellow pencil to check the figures again, but you stop his hand.

"Don't," you say. "It's the same answer."

He puts down the pencil and pushes the tablet aside.

"Sometimes there's a different answer if you look long enough," he says.

"Not this time," you say. "I have to leave tomorrow. So I'm back to the same question. Know anyone that can take me to the bus station?"

Oscar doesn't speak for a minute.

Then he sighs and says, "Yeah. Roger's cousin isn't working. He'll take you. I'll walk over to his house in a little while and ask him."

You wave your hand at the money on the table.

"I got to give this back."

Oscar crosses his arms.

"Can't. That would be an insult," he says.

"All right. Then use it to buy stuff for the next giveaway."

Oscar doesn't say anything. He just picks the money up, a pile at a time and dumps it into a brown paper bag.

A little later, after Oscar has walked over to see Roger's cousin, you hear footsteps in the yard. Someone bangs on the door, and the first thing that you think is that Jack Mason has found you. There's a moment of panic and then a voice hollers, "Oscar! You home?" You think that Jack Mason wouldn't know Oscar's name, probably.

You open the door to Frank Staley. He's standing there in the cold, his breath streaming whiskey scent. He covers his mouth with a brown leather gloved hand, coughs.

"Oscar isn't home right now, Mister Staley."

"Doesn't matter, I really come to see you," he says.

"Me?"

"Yes."

You motion for him to come in. He stomps the snow off his overshoes and steps inside, looking around curiously.

"So, what do you need to talk about? The price gone up?"

"Come on, now, that's not fair. I have to make a living, and there are laws to follow. I can't just—"

"Never mind, never mind. I understand." But you don't.

"It's good news. A third party has agreed to pay for the expenses of transporting the body."

"What? Who?" you ask.

"I'm not at liberty to divulge that. It was a charitable donation, shall we say."

Nancy Marks, you think. Or maybe she got the Catholics to do it, even though Elsie wasn't. But maybe you're not hearing right.

"They're paying for transport, right? What about the vault and the coffin?"

He waves a hand.

"Oh, that, too, that too. And the exhumation order is all signed. If the weather holds, we can exhume the body day after tomorrow. This is Sunday, so you can be on your way by, say, Wednesday afternoon."

You're thinking that there's some good people in this town and some bad ones, too, and all in all, you'll be glad to be gone, long gone. And you're thinking, too, that this town will be glad to have you gone.

"Wednesday? Why not Tuesday afternoon?"

"Goddamn it man, the body had to be removed from the old vault and coffin and placed in a new one, you know. And who knows who might die in the meantime, give me a break. I run the place pretty much by myself."

"Sure, sure," you say. "Okay, Wednesday afternoon."

You're wondering if Roger's cousin can take you to the bus stop on Wednesday instead of tomorrow, but then, Staley says, "You can ride shotgun with the driver. That's a customary courtesy."

You wonder why he didn't have the manners to mention that "customary courtesy" before, but you think about the dollars that are going to stay in your wallet for a little while longer, so you just say, "Thank you."

Staley takes hold of the door knob, and he voices what you've been thinking just a minute ago.

"I don't mind telling you that this town will be glad to put an end to this whole Elsie business. It's been a bad deal from start to finish. Looks like it's about finished."

You want to say that it isn't finished, and will never be as long as whoever killed her isn't known. All that you can hope for is an uneasy peace for yourself and a better resting place for Elsie.

"I figure the crew should have the grave opened around noon on Tuesday if you want to be there," he says as he goes out the door.

February 3, 1970

Digging Up the Past

The yellow machine steadily chews away at the muddy ground, growling like a beast digging out prey from a hiding place. The kerosene ground heater has been moved aside, two men who work part time for Staley stand ready for the final digging, waiting until a third man on the backhoe has cleared away most of the soil. There's a chain coiled loosely to hook onto the vault when the dirt has been removed.

You and Oscar and Nancy sit in her pickup with the heater running. There's a little knot of curious people standing off among the gravestones, watching.

"What I'd like to know is why *he's* here," Nancy says, pointing at the crowd.

"Who?" you ask.

"Packwood," Nancy says. "I suppose he's just come along with those other town nosies hoping that the coffin falls apart and the body fall out so they'll have some disgusting story to tell around their supper tables."

"You didn't have to be here," Oscar tells Nancy.

"Yes, I did," Nancy says. "Whatever happened, she was my friend."

"I don't know as how she was much of a friend," Oscar says. "Considering."

"Well, you know that old saying. A friend in need is a friend indeed," Nancy quotes.

"Not always," Oscar says. "Sometimes a friend in need is a pain in the ass. Or worse."

Nancy's not said a word about the money paid for the body transportation, the new vault, and coffin, but you feel like somebody ought to say something.

"I appreciate what you've done," you say.

"What? Being here? Like I said, in spite of everything, she was my friend."

"I mean," you say, "the money."

Nancy frowns and looks at you.

"What money?"

You can tell that she isn't pretending. She doesn't know what you're talking about.

"Staley is charging a nice chunk of change for transporting the body. I expected that, but I didn't expect to have to pay for a new vault and coffin, too. It was more money than I could get hold of." You don't mention the ghost ceremony or the money collected there to help pay Staley.

"Staley is *charging you*—why that son of a bitch! I'm giving him a piece of my mind!"

She starts to open the pickup door, but you stop her.

"No. No, it's all legal as far as I can tell, although I think he bent the law to put some money in his own pocket. Let it go. Somebody else paid for it. I don't know who. He wouldn't tell me."

Nancy closes the pickup door and puts her mittened hands—pink knitted mittens—in her lap.

"Truth is I couldn't have paid if I had wanted to. Donald didn't have any life insurance, but you can bet that didn't stop Staley from charging me top dollar. In spite of Donald's—well, I couldn't just bury him in a pine box. People would talk. And the ranch has lost money this past year. Most everybody did pretty well, and so did I, but with Donald gone, I had to hire a lot of outside help for work that he used to do."

The three of you are silent for a minute, thinking.

"So, who do you think came up with the cash?" Oscar asks.

Nancy shakes her head.

"I don't know. The good people of this town don't have any money, and the bad ones that have it aren't parting with it, even to get rid of a bad memory."

Oscar nods toward the knot of spectators.

"Maybe Packwood?"

Nancy narrows her eyes.

"Well, he's got the money. But I can't think why he would pay out a dime of it."

The backhoe takes too big of a bite, hits the top of the vault with a crunch.

Nancy winces. The three of you get out and stand as close to the grave as you can while still staying out of the workers' way. It seems appropriate; it seems strange. A funeral in reverse.

Staley waves the backhoe off, and the gravediggers squish through the melted snow and mud, jump down into the hole with their shovels. In a moment they've cleared the rest of the dirt out and attached the chain. The backhoe moves back in and lifts the box. It tilts a little, but the gravediggers rush over, steady it as the backhoe lifts it out, deposits it on a gurney. There are no accidents, no surprises, but the vault has a slightly smashed-in top from where the backhoe dug too deep.

Well, doesn't matter, you think. Had to buy a new vault anyway. Coffin, vault and all are loaded into the back of Staley's hearse, which has been lined with a tarp to protect the interior from the mud. The backhoe operator starts pushing the mud and dirt back into the hole. You watch Staley drive the hearse down the slight grade, turn onto the highway, just as a new black Chevrolet Impala turns off the highway and onto the cemetery road.

"Somebody's late for the party," Oscar says.

The car moves slowly up to the edge of the little crowd. Nancy clutches your arm.

"That car has Mobridge license tags! I bet that's Jack Mason! What the hell is he doing here?"

The driver of the Impala cracks open his car door, gets out and walks towards the three of you, and you're shocked. He's a little man, barely five foot, five inches tall and skinny. He's wearing a silver belly Stetson, starched jeans, and black top coat. His shiny black boots slip a little in the mud. The top of that fancy Stetson *might* come up to your nose. And you were scared of him! But then, you think again. Little men are often underrated, and little men often carry an equalizer, and Jack Mason has his right hand buried in the pocket of that black top coat.

He walks slowly up to the three of you, but he looks right at you. His eyes are that sun-faded blue that's almost white, crinkled around the edges from too much squinting into the wind. He has a nose like a hawk, too big for his small face, and his thin lips are pinched. He may be a small man, but his face says that he gets his way.

"Need to talk to you," he says. "Alone." He starts walking up the incline to a group of tall tombstones.

"I'll come," Oscar says.

Mason turns abruptly, and points at you.

"I just want to talk to him!"

Well, it's broad daylight in front of witnesses. It isn't likely that he's going to kill you. Isn't likely, you tell yourself, as you follow him.

He stops at a pink granite tombstone that's almost as tall as he is.

MARIE ELIZABETH ESTESEN, it reads. And below that a floral wreath encircling the dates: June 10, 1891–October 17, 1959. It's a double tombstone and another name is etched next to hers:

PETER JAMES ESTESEN. But there are no dates below his name.

"Someone you know?" you ask.

Mason looks puzzled, then gets it.

"No, no." He glances at the tombstone as if to make sure, turns back drilling you with those white eyes.

"Look," he says. "I'm just tired of this whole mess. I'm tired of it, you hear? I'm worn completely out with it, and my wife—well," he turns a bit and looks down the hill. "Well, my wife hasn't been the same. She's had a stroke, now. First the boys dying and all."

"I hear that 'the boys' weren't exactly innocents. There are exceptions to that old saying about the good dying young." You're shocked at your own nerve, saying that right out like that, but you're tired, too. You half expect Mason to pull a gun out of that right hand coat pocket and blast you, but he doesn't. He bristles only a little.

"Raising a pair of boys ain't easy! It's this country, it's the times, it's—hell, I don't know—" he waves at the sky. "It's in the weather for all I know! Yeah, I admit, I never had any use for an Indian, and I still don't, but I never taught my boys to be killers or rapists, either. I swear to Christ, I never did that." He subsides for a minute, turns and leans his hand against the tombstone, turns back to face you.

"Christ, you try raising two boys up here," he goes on. "YOU try it! What about your kids? Did you do such a fine job with yours?"

You don't answer. You can't answer. He knows the answer, and you can't look at him. You drop your head.

"Look, man, I know people said I might have done it, that I did it, that my wife was lying to cover for me, but *I swear on my boys' heads, I DID NOT KILL THAT GIRL*. Elsie. I didn't do it. Yeah, I checked it out a few months after my boys died when I started hearing rumors. But I was satisfied that the girl wasn't talking. So I let it alone. I *wanted* to let it alone. Why the hell would I stir it all up again by coming down here and killing that girl?"

You turn back and look at him.

"I don't know. Why would you? Why are you here now?"

He takes a deep breath.

"Do you know what you've done? Do you know? When my wife heard that you were stirring up this whole mess again—well, it just set her off. She's had a stroke, I said. She can't even talk. She just cries, sits in the rest home and cries. I want this *over* with, that's why I'm here. *I want that dead girl and you to hell and gone out of our lives*. You understand? I want an end to this."

"You know, I got a right to be in this, too," you say, "you know it."

"All right," he says, "all right. But is this the end of it? Can I tell my wife it's over? It ain't never going to come up again?"

"As far as I'm concerned," you say. "I'll be taking Elsie out of here tomorrow. But I can't promise what else or who else might bring this up again. You never know what bones someone might dig up."

"And I'll do everything in my power to keep those bones buried," he says.

"You'd do that? Cover up a murder? Cover for a murderer? How do I know you aren't covering for a murderer right now?"

He pulls his hand out of his pocket and the hand is empty, but you think he may actually make a fist and reach up to hit you on the nose with it, but he drops his hand to his side.

"Let it go," he says, and he turns his back to you. "There's been enough dying."

"Yes. There's been too much dying. Too much violence altogether, and it didn't start with Elsie. It began a long time before that."

He doesn't answer for a few minutes, and then he sniffs as if he has a bad cold, reaches into his pocket and pulls out a handkerchief to blow his nose. His voice is thick when he speaks.

"Just take the girl's body and go. Hear me?"

"Gladly," you say, and you walk back to where Oscar and Nancy are waiting beside her pickup.

February 4, 1970

Going Home

It's two o'clock on Wednesday afternoon and you're at the curb in front of Staley's funeral parlor, standing beside the hearse, the driver inside with the motor running. Oscar and Nancy are standing there saying their goodbyes.

"I remember the day I brought her to town," Nancy says. "I think sometimes that I shouldn't have done it, but then where else would she have gone?"

"You did good for her," you say. "Thank you."

Nancy reaches up and hugs you.

"It wasn't enough."

"You did the best you could," you tell her, "can't any human being do more than their best."

You reach out to shake Oscar's hand and he takes your hand in both of his.

"I can't thank you enough," you say.

"Same as I do for any relative," he says. "Same's they would do for me. *You'd* do it for me."

"Yes," you say, "I would. But I still thank you."

"Come back," he says, looking up at the thin veil of snow beginning to fall. "Weather is a lot more pleasant in the summertime."

"I been here in the summertime," you say, "and it ain't."

Oscar's lips lift in a little smile.

"Can't blame a guy for trying."

"You come visit me," you say. "Anytime."

"I don't know as how I'd get along with them civilized Indi'ns."

The hearse driver honks his horn and hollers out the window.

"Storm coming in! If we're going to get out of town, we'd better go now."

You climb into the passenger seat in front, and wave as the driver backs out and starts down the street.

"You mind if I play the radio?" he asks.

"Nope," you say, and you really don't, even when he turns to some rock and roll station playing Elvis Presley. It's alive.

You turn around and glance back at Elsie's coffin in the back, remembering that word that Oscar said to Irene.

Cunksi. Cunksi. We're going home, daughter.

He ha'yela owi'hake.

HIROSHIMA BUGI: ATOMU 57

GERALD VIZENOR

Ronin of Rashomon Gate

Manidoo Envoy

Ronin of the Imperial Moat

Manidoo Envoy

Ronin of the Peace Park

Manidoo Envoy

Ronin of Rashomon Gate

The Atomic Bomb Dome is my Rashomon.

Come closer to the stone, over here, out of the rain. You are the first person to visit me in these ruins. This is my unearthly haven in the remains of the first nuclear war. Only the dead rush their stories under this dome.

The gate of ruins.

The rain, the moody rain, a reminder of that bright and vicious light that poisoned the marrow and forever burned the heart of our memories. Rain, rain, and the ominous stories of black rain. No one can ever be sure of the rain.

The park ravens break that inscrutable silence at the wispy end of a rainstorm. Listen, the shadows of dead children arise from the stone and shout back at the ravens. They mock each other, a parade of ghosts forever teased by the rain.

Sit here, near the ropes.
Twisted reeds?
My kabuki theater.
Raven sumo.
Kabuki of the ruins.
Fierce beauty.
Shadows of the dead.
Ghostly souvenirs.
Atomu war.
Curse of black rain.
Hiroshima by chance.
Kyoto preserved.
Twice by irony.

The Rashomon Gate was in ruins too, more than eight centuries ago. Brutality so old it has turned aesthetic, the fierce cruelty of beauty. We might have been there, waiting for the rain to end just as we are today.

Akutagawa wrote our stories.

Kyoto, a grand city of shrines and willow trees, was wasted, as you know, by natural disasters, war, and wild fires, and that once mighty gate was taken over by animals, thieves, and ghosts.

The warrior ghosts.

Kabuki scenes.

Memory is our gate.

The Atomic Bomb Dome has been registered as a World Heritage. Preserved, as you can see, for the tourists, sentimental bystanders, and, of course, for the cryptic outriders and politicians of peace.

Early in the morning, every morning since this river city was decimated, at this very site, the ruins of the hypocenter, shadows of the dead gather in a ghost parade. The children of incineration, and the white bones of an empire war, arise in a nuclear kabuki theater, and the slender shadows come to light in a ghost parade at eight fifteen, the very same moment of the explosion on August 6, 1945.

My life ended before the bomb.

My life started with the occupation.

My father sent me away.

My father was an army sergeant.

My mother was a cripple.

My mother was a bugi dancer.

My only friends are lepers.

My only friends are orphans.

Our stories are eternal, and the ravens are wise not to break the absolute silence of the ruins in the morning. Stay overnight and you may see a theater of human horseweeds and perfect memories. This is our new story.

Chrysanthemums?

My shirt of tricky shame.

Printed flowers?

Mocks the emperor.

Ruth Benedict?

Story of guilt not shame.

The government poisoned our prized chrysanthemums because of their fear of leprosy. The mere touch of a leper shamed the great beauty of the flowers.

The empire of shame.

Crown stigma.

Sovereignty of the ruins.

My theater is liberty.

Hiroshima arose out of the nuclear ruins to become a testy, prosperous city of peace and victimry. Millions of tourists treasure the origami cranes and forever recite the tragic stories of Sadake Sasaki.

Discovery is the cure.

Never leprosy.

Listen to the distant thunder. The air is thick, heavy, black in the distance. A few days ago lightning struck the dome and demons sizzled down the beams. Have you ever thought about being struck by lightning?

Lightning evades me.

The perfect death is by chance, and the thunderous, terminal turn of a conversation in the rain. The last perfect vision is a burst of bright light, and then the mighty rage of memory.

I pray for lightning.
For death?
Yes, a natural liberty.
Stop praying.
Suddenly, bright, and true.

I was tormented by terrible dreams the first few nights alone here in the ruins. The horror was inescapable. I was caught in the same nightmare, night after night, and could not scare myself awake. The children and lonesome dead crossed over the circle in the ruins.

My nightmare lasted sixty years.

I was surrounded by white bones and burned, puffy bodies. The river was packed with bodies that never floated out to the bay. I was dead, a heap of ancient white bones, and could only reach out for bits of passing flesh to cover my bones, to create a new memory.

> I caught a white pigeon with burned feathers. Suddenly the pigeon turned into an angry ghost and scorned me. Then my bones were mounted in a museum, with my broken, burned watch beside me, probably as punishment for my resistance and tease of time.

My body had deserted me, and my remains were displayed in a diorama of victimry to promote peace. I raged over the passive notions of peace, and then, in the last scene of the nightmare, the museum was destroyed in an earthquake. My bones were liberated by chance and my shadow was cast in a ghost parade, a nuclear kabuki theater. I awakened in the ruins, and every morning since then there has been a ghost parade that starts at eight fifteen ante meridiem.

My body is a nightmare.
Old war wounds?
Yes, but not military.
Samurai?

No, leprosy.

Where?

Oshima, an island of lepers.

Another ghost parade.

The rain is over.

Nasty sores on your face.

The caved nose and sores are the shame, the black rain of culture and disease on my face. No, not the ecstatic fear or perverse pleasures of stigmata. There was nothing aesthetic to bear by reason or creative poses.

My father reported the sores to save my sister from social scorn and separation. No man would have her with a leper brother at home. My face was erased by disease, and my name was erased by fear and family. The police snatched my body and confined me on an island for sixty years, even after there was a cure for leprosy. My war, you see, never ends, there is no surrender, no occupation, no reformation because my body and eroded bones are the ruins of this nasty, cruel, empire culture. My stories are separations of time and family.

Oshima, a perfect nickname.

No, no, too severe.

The samurai of leprosy.

Death in that name.

Tricky stories are liberty.

Try my leprosy.

Oshima of the ruins.

Oshima was my prison, and by torment and desperate loneliness we cared for each other to the end, a wounded and abandoned family. Many of my close friends died of loneliness. Three elders, about my age, and a younger blind woman, the philosophers on the island, died in the same week.

Death by silence.

> For many years we had nurtured prize chrysanthemums on the island. Strong, beautiful flowers gave us courage in the morning. Then, reluctantly, we agreed to cut some of the chrysanthemums for sale in a nearby town, across the Inland Sea.

Happily, the trade developed slowly, but then we were told that our prize chrysanthemums had wilted and died in a single day. My friends died too, outcasts, suicide by desolation, when we learned that the chrysanthemums had been sterilized because we were lepers. Those beautiful blooms died because of our terrible, devoted touch of leprosy.

I reach for the lightning in every storm.

Manidoo Envoy

Ronin Ainoko Browne beat on my door at the Hotel Manidoo in Nogales, Arizona. There was no cause to answer because the sign in the lobby made it perfectly clear that the residents of the hotel were never at home to strangers or solicitors.

Ronin was persistent that morning. I watched him through the eyehole in the door. His moves were theatrical, a measured strut, and his manner cocksure. Open this door, he shouted.

Who are you?

Where is my father?

Not here.

Who are you?

Who is your father?

Sergeant Orion Browne.

Nightbreaker?

Ronin, at first sight, could have been mistaken for Toshiro Mifune. He bounded into the room as if he were on the set of the movie *Rashomon*. He looked around, gestured to the chairs and furniture. Then he turned toward me. My father lives here, he said, over an empty theatrical smile.

Ronin dressed for his father. He wore beaded moccasins, loose black trousers, a pleated shirt shrewdly decorated with puffy white chrysanthemums, and a dark blue cravat. Sadly, he was seven days too late.

Nightbreaker, my best friend, died in his wicker chair near the window. His last gesture was to the raucous ravens perched in the cottonwoods. Ravens inspire natural memories, he told me, and then continued his stories about the tricky imperial ravens in occupied Japan. Ravens create stories of survivance in our perfect memories.

Nightbreaker invited me to move into his room, one of the best in the hotel. We cared for each other as brothers and veterans. That awkward admission soon turned to humor and personal trust. Ronin told me he would stay with his father, late or not, for a few days.

Nightbreaker never mentioned a son, but he told me stories about his lover, Okichi. The name has a grievous history. Japanese authorities, more than a century ago, provided an adolescent by that name as a consort for Townsend Harris, the first consul of the United States. Some prostitutes now bear the same name.

Okichi was a boogie, or *bugi* dancer. "Tokyo Bugi" was the most popular song in the early occupation. Nightbreaker said they first met at a rodeo sponsored by the military and later danced at the Ernie Pyle Canteen in Tokyo. They saw *No Regrets for Our Youth*, directed by Akira Kurosawa, one of the first Japanese films produced after the war. Okichi was not interested in heroic, political stories that were not celebrations of the emperor.

Nightbreaker told me she learned how to kiss in romantic movies and was infatuated by Humphrey Bogart in *Casablanca*. Her favorite song was "Sentimental Journey." Nightbreaker never knew she was pregnant. Okichi disappeared one night and never returned to their regular meeting place at the moat near the Imperial Palace in Tokyo.

Nightbreaker lost his war with cancer, the mortal wounds of his military service. He had been exposed several times to nuclear radiation. If only he had known about his son.

Ronin lived with me, and the memories of his father, for more than a month. The corner room on the second floor overlooked three giant cottonwood trees and the border between Mexico and the United States. He sat in silence for three days in the wicker chair and wrote notes to his father. Then he wore his father's dress uniform and signature cravat every night to dinner and imagined his moves. Ronin learned about the tender manner and sensibilities of his father from the many stories told by other native veterans at the hotel.

Nightbreaker wore the same blue cravat. Naturally, the flourish was familiar, and so was the story. Ronin told us, as his father had years earlier, that their ancestors in the fur trade wore blue to entice women, a practice learned from stories about the wise bower birds who decorate their elaborate nests with something blue. The color is an avian aphrodisiac. Fur traders sold blue cravats to natives, and the myth endures.

Handy Fairbanks founded the Hotel Manidoo some twenty years ago. He is native, a decorated veteran, and once a great hunter on the reservation. Handy lost both of his legs on a land mine, and then the last of his close relatives died in an automobile accident.

Handy created a hotel of perfect memories for wounded veterans. Nightbreaker, who earned his nickname for amorous adventures on the reservation, had lived in the hotel for the past nine years. Many residents thought his distinctive nickname was connected to his military service at nuclear test sites.

Five nights a week we came together for dinner and to create our perfect memories. The marvelous, elusive tease of our many stories, and variations of stories, became concerted memories. Our tricky metaphors were woven together day by day into a consciousness of moral survivance. More than the commerce of reactive survivalists, mere liturgy, ideology, or the causative leverage of a sworn witness, survivance is a creative, concerted consciousness that does not arise from separation, dominance, or concession nightmares. Our stories create perfect memories of survivance.

Natives once named the storiers of the day on trade routes in the canoe country. At night, around a fire, by the signs of natural silence, chance, menace, tricksters, and endurance, the native provenance of stories, were given to perfect memories, and so the wounded veterans of the hotel named a storier of the day.

Nightbreaker was an original native storier, and the tease of his stories became our perfect memories. He touched by totems and metaphors the imagic animals and birds of our survivance. We were always in the bright light of his eternal fires of imagination.

Ronin became a storier, and he mailed his journal to me several years later with vague instructions to provide notes, the necessary descriptive references, and background information on his father and others. The original stories were first scrawled on scraps of paper and later handwritten in seven ledger notebooks.

My personal library, a considerable collection of books about the history, literature, and theater of Japan, aroused his interest in me as a trustee, and he wanted his stories to be associated with his father and the perfect memories of our survivance at the Hotel Manidoo.

Hiroshima Bugi was read out loud at dinner by the storiers named for the day. Ronin would be pleased to hear the creative counts that became part of his tricky stories, and, of course, my commentaries.

Handy, for instance, elaborated on the scenes about romantic movies. Okichi, he said, learned how to dance and tease from *Gone with the Wind*. A copy of the movie was confiscated by soldiers in the Philippines and shown before the end of the war and occupation of Japan. Mister Nightbreaker Butler, when did those nasty soldiers burn Atlanta? Why, Scarlett Okichi, you know it was the Civil War. The Japanese lost the war to the Union.

Handy was a marvelous storier that night, and we honored the perfect memories of Nightbreaker. Clearly, the tricky *renga*, connected scenes, ghost parades, the nuclear kabuki theater in Ronin's *Hiroshima Bugi*, and our imagic bits and riffs, are concerted stories of perfect memories at the Hotel Manidoo.

Oshima Island, or Izu Oshima, a volcanic island, was a prison for lepers near the Izu Peninsula on the Inland Sea. Oshima was recently released from the island after sixty years of separation from society. The sentence and banishment for his disease was sanctioned by the Japanese Leprosy Prevention Law. Many families complied with the law and erased the names of their sons, daughters, and other relatives who were lepers. Oshima, a nickname, lost his real name, his sense of presence, cultural associations, and most of his close friends on the island.

The Atomic Bomb Dome, first protected as a historic site, with no intended irony, is now registered on the World Heritage List. The Sphinx in Egypt, the Great Wall of China, and Grand Canyon National Park, for instance, are also registered as sites of World Heritage.

The Atomic Bomb Dome, near the shore of the Motoyasu River, is the actual ruins of the Hiroshima Industrial Promotion Hall. The Dome, however, is not as real to many tourists as the simulated miniature dome constructed inside the Peace Memorial Museum.

Toyofumi Ogura described the Industrial Promotion Hall in *Letters from the End of the World*. "That old brick building, with its rather exotic dome, was well known in Hiroshima. Though the building was virtually destroyed, roof and floors both having caved in, the steel frame of the dome and the outer walls of the building are still standing. If you step over the rubble and into the remains of the building, you can look up and see the blue sky through the skeleton of the dome, making you feel as if you might be standing amid the ruins of Pompeii."

Ronin declared war on the simulations of peace when he saw, for the first time, the miniature dome over two stories of plaintive peace letters etched on metal plates. Hundreds of reduced metal letters were mounted around a pathetic peace column.

Tadatoshi Akiba, mayor of Hiroshima, for instance, wrote to President William Jefferson Clinton on December 15, 2000. "The United States should look objectively at the history of the 20th Century and realize that nuclear deterrence does not prevent war. Rather, it invites escalation and proliferation of nuclear weapons, thus placing the entire human race at risk of annihilation. Please listen to the international community's sincere desire to eliminate these weapons. Please immediately halt your subcritical nuclear testing, and take your proper place at the forefront of the effort to make the 21st Century free from nuclear weapons." The entire letter is etched on metal, reduced, and mounted on the column of peace. Nearby, there is a letter of protest to Jacques Chirac, president of the French Republic.

Ronin told me he summoned many spectators at the museum and read out loud to them, by shouts and roars, parts of several letters on the column. These letters do not represent peace, but the passive, pathetic apologies for the absence of nuclear weapons. Ronin said the audience rushed to the exits when he announced that the column should be incinerated at the annual peace ceremonies and the country should bear nuclear weapons.

"Peace is the order, however imperfect, that results from agreement between states, and can only be sustained by that agreement," wrote Michael Howard in *The Invention of Peace*. Peace is "not an order natural to mankind: it is artificial, intricate and highly volatile." Japan would reach a better agreement on peace if the military possessed nuclear weapons to protect the peace, said Ronin. Peace is not a column of mundane letters to heads of state. The peace museums and souvenir counters only weaken the stories of nuclear survivance.

Akutagawa Ryunosuke published the story "Rashomon" in 1915. *Rashomon* the movie was actually based on another story, "In a Grove," and directed by Akira Kurasawa. "Rashomon" the story is set in twelfth-century Kyoto.

"The Atomic Bomb Dome is my Rashomon," wrote Ronin. The allegory of the first line of his journal, the short story, and the film, starts in the rain. Akutagawa's story opens with the servant of a samurai and an old woman in the twelfth century. The servant becomes a thief and the old woman tears hair from corpses that are dumped at Rashomon Gate in Kyoto. Ronin's journal opens with an orphan and a leper in the Atomic Bomb Dome in Hiroshima.

Akutagawa and Ronin are poets of disasters. Ronin created a ceremonial circle with a rope of twisted reeds in the tradition of sumo and the kabuki theater. Misery and mischance are exorcised by entering the circle, and, as he reveals later, by stomping on a picture of the emperor. The many corpses at the gate in the twelfth-century story are the shadows and nuclear dead of today.

That metaphor, human horseweeds, is borrowed from stories told by the *hibakusha*, the survivors, of the first flowers to bloom after the nuclear destruction of Hiroshima.

Ronin creates dialogue in a kabuki theater style, short, direct, positional words and sentences. He never discussed the style of his scenes, shifts of pronoun, transformations, or metaphorical tease, but he was strongly influenced by kabuki and sumo theater. Ronin created from perfect visual memory a theatrical, literary style. The characters, as in the scene with the leper, could be transposed in a nuclear allegory.

"Kabuki has attained its own blend of reality and unreality. It has created its own flavor which derives from hovering in its own way between the two poles. It now remains only a matter for the spectator to draw delight from the result," wrote

Faubion Bowers in *Japanese Theater*. "There are moments on the stage of complete and literal representation of reality, followed by such fancy as to border on the nonsensical. Sometimes through the vast art resources available to kabuki, a perfect illusion is created, independent either of reality or of methods of creating fiction. Often this illusion is deliberately broken by the insertion of passages which of necessity force the spectator back into an awareness of himself and reminds him that what he has been seeing is merely a stage performance. For example, often actors will refer to themselves or to other actors in the course of the play by their names."

The kabuki theater is a measured transcendence of the obvious. The sound of *hyoshigi*, clacker sticks, and the curtain opens on a trace of sumo wrestlers, the circles, and narrow approach to the arena and stage. "Not only is the stylization of gestures and the marking out of ceremonial space common to both sumo and kabuki, but both performances also feature ceremonial stamping," wrote Yamaguchi Masao in "Sumo in the Popular Culture of Contemporary Japan."

Ronin posed in his black trousers and chrysanthemum shirt, sounded the *hyoshigi*, he told me, and created a nuclear kabuki theater in the registered haven of cultural shame, The Atomic Bomb Dome. His theatrical tease was nuclear, not feudal, and by his tricky moves the illusions of peace were converted into stories of survivance. He was a teaser, not an appeaser, of nuclear peace.

The Peace Memorial Museum created the simulations that dominate the international politics of nuclear peace, and by boosters, souvenirs, and ritual tours weaken the traditional art of war and creative nuclear survivance.

The Japanese would rather rebuild a shrine as a traditional ritual than preserve a shrine, so the preservation of nuclear ruins is an ironic gesture. The ruins are true, beyond ritual preservation. Ronin pointed this out and announced at the annual peace party that the possession of nuclear weapons is a ritual balance, a traditional renewal of peace. Japan rebuilds shrines, why not peace by nuclear weapons?

"Preserving material objects is not the only way to conserve a heritage," wrote David Lowenthal in *The Past Is a Foreign Country*. "The great Ise Shinto temple in Japan is dismantled every twenty years and replaced by a faithful replica built of similar materials exactly as before. Physical continuity signifies less to the Japanese than perpetuating the techniques and rituals of re-creation." The techniques of peace, then, are ritual power and persuasion, and an active peace is created by the possession and renewal of nuclear weapons, not by passive memorials. Ask any samurai warrior about peace, shouted Ronin.

Ronin, by his presence in the ruins, created a ritual, a nuclear kabuki theater that teased and defied the preservation of peace. The Peace Memorial Museum, at the same time, constructed a theme park miniature of the Atomic Bomb Dome.

The kabuki theater is a ritual trace of the feudal past, the rue and craze of loyalty. "Kabuki seems to me to have the perfect balance between the sensuality and ritual which are the two poles of Japanese culture," wrote Alex Kerr in *Lost Japan*. "At the same time, there is a tendency in Japan towards overdecoration, towards cheap sensuality too overt to be art. Recognizing this, the Japanese turn against the sensual. They polish, refine, slow down, trying to reduce art and life to its pure essentials. From this reaction were born the rituals of tea ceremony, Noh drama and Zen. In the history of Japanese art you can see these two tendencies warring against each other."

Ronin was at war with traditions and simulations of peace, and in a mighty theater pose he advanced the outrageous idea of more nuclear weapons for peace and called for a supranational soldiery to enforce a nuclear peace. He borrowed that general idea from Albert Einstein, who wrote that mankind "can only gain protection against the danger of unimaginable destruction and wanton annihilation if a supranational organization has alone the authority to produce or possess these weapons." Einstein prepared that obscure message for the Peace Congress of Intellectuals at Wroclav in 1948.

Ronin boldly declared that the Japanese must vote to amend their constitution so the government can possess nuclear weapons as a theatrical balance of crucial, reductive rituals and pleasures. The nuclear kabuki theater is a ghost parade and the aesthetic symmetry of erotic power. Ronin surely lost his audience with these comments about a nuclear-armed soldiery.

Ronin of the Imperial Moat

Ronin is my name, as you know, and he has no parents to bear his stories, no memorable contours, creases, or manner of silence at night. My name is wild, a nuclear orphan, a samurai warrior without a master to exact my loyalty.

My parents are shadows.

That me of creation is the face of the other, the virtual you by my absence, and now we come to the same aesthetic vengeance of pronoun closures. You never had a calendar of promises, or cultural service, nothing to remember by the sanguinary rights of way. My father, the touch of you is mythic, the tease of our nature is forever in my story.

> My parents might have posed for me in that photograph, the only trace of their romance and my conception. My father is set in his uniform, a sergeant and interpreter for the occupation army. He could have been an actor in the kabuki theater. I hear him at night in that theatrical voice. My mother wears a print dress decorated with giant chrysanthemums. She has a shy, coy smile, the coquette of romantic movies, a fugitive of war in *Casablanca*. Nightbreaker was her Humphrey Bogart. I was conceived there, in the grassy background of that snapshot, on the banks of the moat outside the Imperial Palace.

My royal conception.

> Ronin must be my name, an orphan of the ruins outside the imperial moat. My only association is a snapshot simulation,

> and the evidence of my conception is an emulsive document. No dates, no records, and no relatives to celebrate my first, sudden breath in the world. Yet, the animistic stories of my survivance are perfect memories.

Death is my vision in the faint morning light. The master said, We are separated from a sense of presence because of our fear of death. Consider the instance of nuclear wounds every morning and the fear of death vanishes. The samurai warrior is never shamed by the fear of death.

> My first death was by chance, a high fever at the orphanage. Great ravens crashed through the windows in a burst of brilliant light. Suddenly, my feathers, yes my feathers, turned black and we soared over paddy fields and circled Mount Fuji.

I could see the orphanage in the distance and blue shivers of waves on the bay. We soared over docks, bridges, ceremonies, and military camps in the ruins of great cities. Many kabuki actors posed at a distance in traditional costumes. Tokyo, to the north, was an expanse of shanties and mounds of ashes. The Oasis of Ginza and the Imperial Palace were standing alone in the ruins of war.

> My father was there, an interpreter for the occupation army. We soared over the imperial moat and my father watched me circle and dive right past his shoulder. My mother, in the abundant reign of the emperor, leaned back under the course of raucous ravens, raised those puffy chrysanthemums, and conceived an ainoko boy, me, on the moist grassy bank of that moat.

My second death was staged seven years later. Those vivid scenes of ravens last night after night. I could not resist the wonder and lust of the ruins and ran away to Tokyo. Most of the shanties were gone and the streets were cleared. The new public buildings obstructed some views of Mount Fuji. I camped for three nights in the memory of my parents, as they had appeared to me in my death dream as a raven. Many soldiers and bugi dancers were on the moat that night.

> I stood in the same place my father watched me soar over his shoulder. The imperial ravens circled overhead and teased me on that grassy mound near the moat, the actual site of my conception in the wicked reign of the emperor. The ravens strutted on the empire bridge, bounced and croaked in the secure trees. My tatari, raven vengeance, in a nuclear theater.
>
> I am memory, the destroyer of peace.
> I am time, the vengeance of fake peace.
> I am the father, a perfect memory.
> I am death, the apparition of peace.

The idea of peace is untrue by nature, a common counterfeit of nations, but the most treasonous peace is based on nuclear victimry. There is no more treacherous a peace than the nuclear commerce of the Peace Memorial Museum in Hiroshima.

> I am dead, the one who shatters nuclear peace. Some of my deaths have been reported in obituaries around the world. Dead Amerika Indian, hafu peace boy out to sea, was the report of my second death at the orphanage. I am forever an orphan, a tatari of the ruins, and the curse of commerce in the name of nuclear peace.

Okichi praised the emperor in her renunciation note to the orphanage. The emperor was the very cause of her deceptions of paradise. She could not protect or nurture an ainoko, a hafu, or halfbreed child, born of the erotic sensibilities of the occupation. She did not mention my father by name, only by occupation, a translator, and by simulation, Amerika Indian who worked with Faubion Bowers and General Douglas MacArthur.

> My father was almost there, only seven days short of my awkward presence at the hotel and my movie rush to overbear the absence of a natural touch of paternity. I wore my chrysanthemum shirt to remind him of his lover, my mother, the bugi dancer in a lost empire. My stories create perfect memories of my father.

I am dead once more, my most memorable samurai signature. The person you see has become a raven, a bear, a sandhill crane of anishinaabe totems. The nuclear orphan is a ronin, out of time, and with no crisscross of ancestors to avow and avoid in the ordinary.

> The nature of my conception is imagic, the lost art of romance by the occupation, bugi dancers, the miniature emperor, and motion pictures. My resistance is more to manners, hand towels, the cast of mean cultural burdens, and amenable bows than to fate. Chance is my perfect sovereignty. My samurai loyalty, as an ainoko ronin, is to those who are menaced and demeaned by the decorous, unbearable commerce of nuclear peace. My vengeance as a tatari is for those who shame the nuclear dead with souvenirs of peace.

The simulations of nuclear peace will be complete when the hibakusha, the atomic bomb survivors, wear souvenir tee shirts with messages such as, "Hiroshima Loves Peace," or the entreaty "No More Hiroshima, August 6, 1945, A Day to Remember, Atomic Bombing of Hiroshima," or the understated "Hiroshima, A-Bomb Dome," with letters turned awry, as if the last two words had been cutely bombed. Tourists wear these vacuous shibboleths in the Peace Memorial Museum.

> I mocked the awry worded tee shirt once at the museum and promised autographs to every tourist. The shop sold twice as many shirts that day, and no one, not even the

peacemongers, caught the cruel irony of my autograph. I signed the name Paul Tibbets on each white shirt in bold cursive letters.

I wore my favorite tee shirt only once in the museum. Printed on the front, sleeve to sleeve, was a famous question about the atomic bomb, Is it big enough? The museum security guards teased me because they thought it was a gesture to my penisu. I never wore it again in public.

The Peace Memorial Museum is a pathetic romance, a precious token to honor the state memory of a culpable emperor, as my mother might have done, with a sensuous, passive, origami pose of occupation victimry. Peace is the tease of the nuclear war no one dares to declare.

The Atomic Bomb Dome might have been the death of my father. He was an army interpreter with the advance occupation forces at the end of the war and traveled with investigators and photographers to Hiroshima.

Near here, in my nuclear kabuki theater of the ruins, he was exposed to nuclear radiation, and twenty years later he was diagnosed with cancer. Hiroshima he might have survived, had he not been ordered a few years later to witness nuclear tests at Yucca Flat in Nevada. He retired from the army, nursed his nuclear wounds, and built a cabin at the headwaters of the Mississippi River near the White Earth Reservation in Minnesota. He recovered by meditation, native medicine, and the annual stories of survivance at the headwaters. Later, after many years as a roamer, he moved south with two other wounded veterans to the Hotel Manidoo in Nogales, Arizona.

My samurai deaths are traced by chance, by the occupation, the tricks and ironies of romance, and by eternal solitude, that elusive disease of orphans. The ainoko orphans with the disease are seldom deceived by the politics and commerce in nuclear souvenirs at the Peace Memorial Museum.

> The courage of a samurai warrior is hidden, his loyalty a tease, untested, wasted in a culture of simulated peace. The new political masters are separated by manners and comp romised by the commerce of peace and victimry.

Manidoo Envoy

Ronin is the invincible samurai of his marvelous stories, the eternal teaser with a vacant smile, a simulated death pose. By his account he has been dead and buried seventeen times in the past decade.

Mifune, his nickname at the orphanage, vanished once as a raven in a fever vision, as you know, and his second death was staged, a swimming accident at Oiso Long Beach on Sagami Bay. "Orphan of Destiny Drowns in the Bay," might have been a headline story, but a week later a teacher found him on the Ginza in Tokyo. Who, at the time, would not run away to the Ginza?

Mifune vanished by tricky maneuvers, a strategic death, and an imagic rise in another name and place. This was not an unusual practice because the Japanese do the same thing for economic reasons. The common ruse is known as a "midnight run," a change of identities arranged by a third party. Thousands of people "disappear each year," wrote Alex Kerr in *Dogs and Demons*. "They discard their homes, change their identities, and move to another city, all to hide from the enforcers of Japan's consumer loans."

Mifune was entranced by scenes of *Chushingura*, and later *Genji Monogatari*, at the Kabukiza Theatre in Tokyo. He had a perfect memory of the scenes, and on the way back to the orphanage he described in visual detail the music, costumes, gestures, hairstyles, and cosmetics of the actors. He tormented his teachers by beating the *hyoshigi*, or clacker sticks, to announce his orphan play.

I was stationed there at about the same time, in the late fifties, as a legal investigator for the Army. I might have been at the very same theater with the orphan Mifune.

Nightbreaker had been reassigned ten years earlier, but even so we shared many stories and created our perfect memories of Japan. We were both *anishinaabe*, but from different reservations. I am a member of the Leech Lake Reservation, and he lived to the west, on the White Earth Reservation. The *anishinaabe* were named the Ojibwe and Chippewa.

Nightbreaker was an interpreter for the first year or so of the occupation, and then, because of his experience with investigators at Hiroshima, he was assigned to Camp Desert Rock, a nuclear test site in Nevada.

Reason Warehime had similar experiences in Nagasaki and at the Nevada Test Site. He and Nightbreaker participated in atomic test site maneuvers. Reason noticed "when you get out closer that a lot of the sand had kind of melted into a glaze, like a brown glass. Then we got sunburn, and the guys all started throwing up in the truck going back," he told Carole Gallagher in *American Ground Zero*. Nightbreaker, Reason, and many other men lost their teeth and hair after the test. "It started every time you put your comb through your hair, you come out with a big gob of hair," said Reason. "It would have been three years later when they finally had to pull every tooth in my mouth because they had all turned black and came real loose."

The Nevada Test Site was their Rashomon.

The Kabukiza Theatre was destroyed at the end of the war and rebuilt in 1951. Faubion Bowers was first moved by the artistic tradition and then obsessed with the eminence of the kabuki actors. The first production he saw was *Chushingura* at the Kabukiza Theatre a year before the attack on Pearl Harbor. When he returned five years later, and two weeks after the surrender, as an officer and interpreter with the advance forces of the occupation, he had kabuki theater on his mind. The Japanese newspaper reporters and nervous officials were surprised when Bowers asked them about a famous kabuki actor, "Is Uzaemon still alive?"

Ichimura Uzaemon XV, "the leading *kabuki* actor of his generation, had died of a sudden heart attack" three months earlier, wrote Shiro Okamoto in *The Man Who Saved Kabuki*. Bowers said Uzaemon was his favorite actor, "the kind of star who could stir people up about anything. He was a legendary *kabuki* actor." Uzaemon is one of the oldest and most traditional names in the theater.

Bowers intervened to protect the kabuki theater from closure by the occupation. Military censors had reduced the great kabuki tradition to a tincture of feudalism, a dangerous art. Bowers, by his advertence, aesthetic enterprise, and compassion saved kabuki. He even brought food to the hungry actors in the early months of the occupation. Japan "has maintained in a living form most of the traditions of her earlier theaters," Bowers wrote five years later in his first book, *Japanese Theater*.

"Amidst the prohibitions of the postwar period, it was Bowers who expanded the range of permissible actors and plays," observed Ichimura Uzaemon XVII. "His existence was crucial. It was especially crucial for *kabuki*."

Mifune, by chance, saw Ichimura Uzaemon XVII years later in a production of *Chushingura*, or *The Treasury of Loyal Retainers*. Kabuki stage names are either inherited or bestowed. Uzaemon, Bowers, Nightbreaker, Mifune, and this storier are connected by chance and the perfect memories of kabuki theater.

Mifune was never the same after first seeing *Chushingura*, and then *Genji Monogatari* at the Kabukiza Theatre. He told me that he had already decided to live by more than one name and that he staged his death to defy the obvious outcome of an *ainoko* orphan in Japan. The kabuki theater inspired him, as it had his father and me, and he created spectacular turns of chance, funerals, and created many new identities.

Okichi might have named her son Atomu, for "atomic," as no other name was revealed. There are no public records of his birth; however, he has created a record of death in various names. Atomu was a teaser name at the orphanage, but he was soon given the name of the actor, Mifune. The name was inspired by the actor's scruffy nature, empty smile, and the surly, confident gestures of a samurai warrior. Mifune the orphan would more than consummate the nickname.

Toshiro Mifune appeared in several movies at the time. He was a yakuza in *Drunken Angel*, and he played the role of a bandit in *Rashomon*, directed by Akira Kurosawa. "Mifune has no drive for perfection, he has a drive for virtue," wrote Donald Richie in *Public People, Private People*. Mifune, the runaway orphan, on the other hand, had no earthly drive for virtue, compared to the actor, but he had a mighty desire for perfect memories.

Ronin was the nickname he earned after his adoption on the White Earth Reservation. The tribal council conferred his surname in memory of his father, Orion Browne. Ronin, as you know, created a gutsy visionary presence and perfect memory of his father at the Hotel Manidoo.

Bowers and Nightbreaker first met in military language school at Camp Savage in Minnesota. Bowers was drawn to the language because of his prewar experiences in Japan. Nightbreaker learned about haiku poetry from a Benedictine monk at the mission school on the reservation. Later he studied Japanese on his own for several years because he was fascinated by the adventures of Ranald MacDonald, who was a native and, ironically, the first teacher of English in Japan. Nightbreaker had prepared to make the very same journey, more than a century later, but instead he enlisted, at the start of the war, in the Army. He spoke *anishinaabe*, which was not of much value to the military, and to prove his basic competence in Japanese he recited by memory several haiku poems and scenes from "Rashomon," a story by Akutagawa Ryunosuke. Father and son were inspired by the same authors and by kabuki theater.

Ronin, the son of an interpreter, carried out his father's vision and traced the enterprise of MacDonald from Ainu communities in Hokkaido to Nagasaki. He created perfect memories of his father on the road of visions, and that was how he returned with his father, a visionary union, to Japan.

Ronin was determined to find his parents, but he had only a note and photograph to represent his family. These rather cryptic documents were attached to his clothes when he was abandoned, apparently by his mother, at the Elizabeth Saunders Home. He was about two years old at the time and had no memory of his mother.

Ronin created a new era calendar to name the year of his surrender, the tricky reign of the *ainoko* orphans. Atomu 3, on the atomic *gengo* calendar, marked the reign of nuclear peace, or the number of years since Little Boy, the first atomic bomb, destroyed Hiroshima. His system mocked the imperial reign of the emperors, Showa for Hirohito, Heisei for Akihito. "This marriage of calendar to sovereign is not a traditional way of counting time in Japan, but rather a highly modern way of engaging in symbolic politics," wrote John Dower in *Japan in War and Peace*.

Okichi wrote, "atomu ainoko, jugatsu 1946, amerika indian chichi worku by babinu bowu to macatu." She meant, of course, that her son was born a *hafu* in October 1946, his father was American Indian, and he worked with Major Faubion Bowers, the interpreter and assistant military secretary to General Douglas MacArthur, Supreme Commander of the Allied Powers. Nightbreaker was in the same occupation unit as Bowers. They were close friends from Camp Savage.

Mifune and thousands of *ainoko*, or *hafu* children, were the untouchables of war and peace in two countries. Japan would never embrace the progeny of the occupation, and his father had no idea that he existed. The United States, at the same time, enacted very restrictive immigration laws. Mifune was actually adopted by the tribal government at the White Earth Reservation.

"Getting permission for half-Japanese adopted children to enter the United States was extremely difficult because of the racial exclusion provision of the immigration laws," observed Yukiko Koshiro in *Trans-Pacific Racisms*. "The task facing Japan was to find a way to assimilate this 'inferior' racial group into society. The absence of their American fathers made their situation different from other minority groups."

Mifune was one of many "Orphans of Destiny" at the Elizabeth Saunders Home at Oiso, a town south of Kamakura on Sagami Bay. Miki Sawada established the orphanage about three years after the end of the war. She was related to the founder of Mitsubishi, and her husband, an ambassador before the war, was a representative to the United Nations.

Sawada "remained the foremost advocate of the separation policy, which she believed would protect the children's 'mental and physical handicaps' from the hostile outside world. Only in a shielded world would they learn to gain self-esteem and become strong and secure," wrote Yukiko Koshiro.

Mifune, and the other orphans, studied two languages to endure as *ainoko* in two cultures. Sawada taught the children to "serve as a future link of the two nations." Ronin would be more than a dubious, tractable connection of separatist nations. He would establish a nuclear kabuki theater in the ruins and forever haunt the obedient peacemongers.

The Japanese Ministry of Welfare declared that there were some five thousand mixed-blood children born during the first few years of the occupation of Japan. Others were convinced there were as many as two hundred thousand children fathered by occupation soldiers.

Mifune was fortunate that he was abandoned at the Elizabeth Saunders Home. The nurses and teachers were both sensitive and strong, but a generation later he would overturn the passive notions of peace that he had once been taught.

Sawada was a dedicated, honorable humanist, and persuasive in the world, but she could not overcome government resistance to more liberal adoption policies for orphans.

Military investigators finally identified the errant sergeant in the photograph and located his last residence. Nightbreaker had retired with a medical disability after fifteen years of active service. When the military assumed he had died of radiation disease the orphanage negotiated with tribal leaders at the White Earth Reservation. Nightbreaker was highly respected for his sense of tradition. He was a native speaker of *anishinaabe*, a great storier, and was honored for his military service.

The White Earth Reservation petitioned federal officials to set aside immigration laws and allow a native child to return to his family. Mifune was an unusual adoption, as the tribal government had the support of the state delegation in Congress. Mifune Browne, as he was named in the petition, an *anishinaabe* and Japanese orphan, age fifteen, was adopted by special legislation and without a specific family. Congress was eager to please tribal officials because they wanted easy access to natural resources on the reservation.

Mifune, and then Ronin, is a citizen of Japan and the United

States. His adoption was political, not familial, and so he remains a citizen by birth of Japan.

Japan was forever in his memories, a road of chance not to be taken twice, but then he learned of his father's vision, alas, too late to recover the touch of his humor, here at the Hotel Manidoo.

"I am memory, the destroyer of peace," wrote Ronin. Surely he mocked J. Robert Oppenheimer, the nuclear physicist and director of the Los Alamos Laboratory. Oppenheimer had studied scriptures in Sanskrit and remembered a verse from the Bhagavad-Gita, "I am become Death, the destroyer of worlds," after the first atomic bomb test at the Trinity site near Alamogordo, New Mexico. Ronin was aware of at least two translations of the Bhagavad-Gita. Kees Bolle translated the same verse, "I am Time who destroys man's world." Stephen Mitchell's version, "I am death, shatterer of worlds, annihilating all things," slightly alters the tone. Ronin wrote that he was time, memory, and death, the destroyer of the pretense of nuclear peace. He would destroy the nuclear peace simulations at the Peace Memorial Museum.

Colonel Paul Tibbets was the pilot of the *Enola Gay*, the plane that released Little Boy, the first atomic bomb, over Hiroshima. For that he received the Distinguished Service Cross on his return to the airbase at Tinian Island in the South Pacific.

Niels Bohr asked J. Robert Oppenheimer at Los Alamos, "Is it big enough?" Mary Palevsky commented on the context of that question in her book *Atomic Fragments*. Hans Bethe explained in a conversation on nuclear arms control that the question meant, is the bomb "big enough to make war impossible?"

Ronin borrowed the idea of peace as the "nuclear war no one dares to declare" from *The Invention of Peace* by Michael Howard. "It has often been said that between 1945 and 1989 peace was kept by a war that nobody dared to fight."

Ronin adapted the phrase "the abundant reign of the emperor" from the *norito*, the ancient traditions, rituals, and prayers of Shinto. The Hirano Festival contains the entreaty "All these various offerings do I place, raising them high like a long mountain range, and present. Receive, then, tranquilly, I pray, and these noble offerings; Bless the reign of the Emperor as eternal and unmoving, Prosper it as an abundant reign."

The *tatari* are spirits of retribution and vengeance, a curse of kami, a spirit of nature and ancestors. The "Japanese had feared the *tatari* of the dead, that is, the vengeance of people who had been killed, or killed themselves, after being falsely accused or unfairly treated," Maurice Pinguet wrote in *Voluntary Death in Japan*. "The vengeful could persecute its enemies, strike at the innocent in passing, and unleash all manner of scourges."

Donald Richie described the firebombed wasteland of Tokyo in 1947. Mount Fuji was visible, one winter day early in the occupation, from the Ginza. "Between me and Fuji was a burned wasteland, a vast and blackened plain where a city had once stood," he wrote in his journal, later published in *The Donald Richie Reader*. "Mount Fuji stood sharp on the horizon, growing purple, then indigo in the fading light," he observed. The Kabukiza Theatre and Mitsukoshi Department Store were in ruins, but the mountain was resplendent. "Fuji looked much as it must have for Hokusai and Hiroshige."

Mount Fuji, a mighty, natural spirit, remains the same, only the views have changed since the occupation. Mifune would have had a similar view of the mountain when he ran away from the orphanage. The Ginza today is a wild, postmodern, international trade center.

Ronin of the Peace Park

Atomu 57 on my calendar of fake peace. This is my promissory time, eight fifteen, my gate of giveaway souls, and my rites of passage in the ruins of the Atomic Bomb Dome. Remember the abundant reign of the emperor in the era of nuclear peace. The ghost parade is my tricky empire of Rashomon Gate.

> I poured gasoline on the Pond of Peace at the Peace Memorial Museum. Thin, elusive ribbons caught the morning light and spread across the water in magical hues. The phantom plumes reached out from the Cenotaph and almost touched the Flame of Peace.

I counted the seconds and threw a lighted match into the water at eight fifteen of the hour, the start of the ghost parade. The fire burst, tumbled, and roared over the pond. That moment was a tribute to natural reason and perfect memories.

> The fire wavered, curved higher, bounced downwind, and never once licked back at my hand. The flames that seared the fake peace that morning last forever. Shadows, faint traces of a ghost parade, were burned on the concrete containment walls around the pond. The mighty ravens croaked at a great distance.

A fire engine arrived a few minutes later, and then the police searched the area. I waited near the ruins, on the stone stairs to the river, and cast fresh cucumbers into the dark water to tease and appease the nanazu tricksters. The police questioned the roamers who were camped on the other side of the river. I shouted my hafu nickname and waved at the police. They stared back at me and then bowed slightly. The roamers were amused and waved wildly.

> I became a sandhill crane, and bounced with my wings trimmed close to the side, and danced down the stones to the riverside. My forehead turned reddish, and my dance turns were erotic and crazy.

Oshima was touched by my dance, but he warned me to be cautious, more discrete around the police. They shame by turns of sympathy, he told me, and they have too much authority. You have none, ainoko of the ruins, and the roamers watched you light the sacred pond this morning.

Little Boy souvenirs.
Not a wise story.
Roamers are storiers.
Yes, and twicers.
Who would listen?
The police.
Not by stories.
Always by story.
What stories?
The leper story.
Empire evidence.
No, fear by story.
So many, many versions.

> Several roamers on the other side of the river leaned out and pointed in our direction. I shouted my hafu nickname once more and danced at the riverside. The police radioed for assistance and then hurried across the Aioi Bridge. The ravens soared over the river, circled the police, and then perched on the skeleton beams in the ruins.

The police discovered the ghostly shadows on the wall around the Pond of Peace. They sighed for shame, public shame, and then copied each shadow into a notebook. There was no other evidence of a fire or trace of the cause. The stories of the fire were elusive.

> Suddenly, several police cars were on the scene. They asked our names, our residences, and continued, respectfully, with the usual manner of an interrogation. Oshima refused to speak because of his memories of betrayal. The last time he dared to trust the police he was removed from his world, his family, and with no medical or legal consideration sentenced to a leprosarium for sixty years.

The police might have shouted to threaten his silence, but instead avoided him when they discovered his blunt fingers and the sores on his face. They shunned the leper, secured their white gloves, and surrounded me. I resisted by shouting my nicknames, and refused to speak Japanese.

> You namae.
> No, no.
> No namae.
> Yes, name.
> You namae.
> Atomu Ainoko.
> You adana.
> Mifune.
> No adana.
> Ronin Browne.
> No adana.
> Take my soul.

> Oshima was ordered to leave the area and never return. He boldly refused to move, and sat in silence on the stone stairs to the river. Tosuto, the mongrel, and three ravens waited nearby. I was detained at last in the back of a police car.

Kitsutsuki, that surly veteran with a wooden leg, and several other roamers rushed over the bridge and tried to intervene, but the police would not listen to their stories. They were very worried about us, and they told me that the police had abused their generosity and distorted their gestures and stories. Kitsutsuki executed a mighty frown, and he was famous for his frowns. He told the police that we might know, but not as perpetrators, who was responsible for the fire on the Pond of Peace.

> I was taken to a koban, a police post a few blocks away near the river, but was never arrested. The koban was surrounded by giant sunflowers, and on the inside, every windowsill and counter was decorated with potted plants. The post had a strong scent of mold, probably from the soil in hundreds of pots. Out back in a shed there were bicycles, a piano, a golf bag, giant ceramic pots, many lost or abandoned objects, and several wooden legs.

Osaka, a former catch girl, told me later that she has favored the local koban for several years. By favor she meant tea and flowers. She was grateful to the police for their discrete protection at a time when yakuza creditors were in pursuit. She moved from another city, a midnight run, to avoid high interest debts. The debt was paid in time, and since then she has dutifully served teas and decorated the tiny post with flowers. Surely she would have done something else if the senior officer had not been secretly in love with flowers, or as many neighbors might say, covertly in love with the bearer of the flowers.

> I was directed to sit in a sturdy, straight, and narrow wooden chair, stationed in the center of the room and in front of a shiny metal desk. The light shimmered through the windows. I removed my coat, and the police pointed at the words on my tee shirt.
>
> > What mean?
> > Bomb, big enough?
> > What bomb?
> > Atomu bakudan.

I raised my hands, puffed my cheeks, traced the shape of a

mushroom cloud in the air, and then pointed to the words on my chest, Is it big enough?

> The police stared at me, lighted cigarettes, and then turned away in silence. They were gentle and friendly at first, and then apologetic for the delay. An interpreter had been summoned from the central police station.

The real fun started when the police interpreter arrived in a huge van, a mobile koban. The van wheezed to the curb, the doors cracked open, and a tiny woman leaped out. Tonase was dressed to the nines in a blue uniform. The short black visor of her peaked hat rode low and almost covered her eyes. The gold star on the peak of her hat shined in the morning light.

> She pointed at the words, one by one, on my tee shirt, looked to the side, blushed, and then said something about the size of my penisu in Japanese. The other police were stunned by her comment, and then they burst into laughter.

The police misunderstand the message, but it was too late to explain the history. I laughed only to rescue my sense of presence and pointed at her socks as she crossed her legs behind the desk. The bright white socks were trimmed with bloated cartoon images of cats and chickens. She wagged one foot and stared at me.

Please, your names.
Your names?
Yes, your names.
Ainoko Mifune Ronin Browne.
Japanese citizen?
Big laugh.
Amerika name?
Nickname, adana.
Yes, adana?
Mifune.
Clan name?

Big laugh.

You citizen?

Born ainoko, an orphan.

Please, you ages.

You ages?

Yes, you ages.

Atomu fifty six.

What time?

Fifty six in the ruins.

Mister Browne, we know you are ainoko, and we respect you, but you left many years ago, a hafu adopted by Amerika Indians in United States. You stay, never return to Japan.

Japan is my country.

How you return?

By Ainu.

By who?

Ainu in Hokkaido.

Ainu shaman.

No Ainu.

Ainu boaters.

You joke me.

Yes, yes, but truly.

The cats and chickens vanished as she uncrossed her legs. She leaned to the side and told the others about the minority boaters in Japanese. The police looked at each other, then at me, and laughed politely.

You joke everyone.

Yes, by irony.

Ainu gone.

Not the bears.

Now, where you live?

Rashomon Gate.

Please, no jokes.
I live with a leper in the ruins.
What leper?
Oshima, the kabuki leper.
What ruins?
Atomic Bomb Dome.
You joke me again.
Big enough?
No jodan, joke.
You hear my tease.
Amerika tease?
Tease of interrogatory.
Who are you?
Samurai warrior.
No, no sense.
Bushido survivance.
No jodan.
Buy my soul.
What soul?
Samurai soul.
No buy.
Take my soul.

The courage and loyalty of a samurai warrior remains hidden, never tasted, the savor wasted in a time of sentimental, simulated peace and victimry.

Suddenly, the show of courtesy had ended in the koban. She raised her right hand, pointed, and shouted at me. The sympathetic manner of initial police interrogations had turned to verbal abuse, but the pitch of her voice was not convincing. My resistance was by tease and irony, not by deceptive tactics and practices. The police, as usual, would never believe that my ironic confessions and stories were true. So, my best defense was a tricky style of sincerity.

Now, where you sleep?

National treasure.

On street?

Nuclear ruins.

Where?

Ground zero.

Why wooden sword?

Honor my nanazu.

What name?

The nanazu water tricksters.

You crazy.

Take my soul.

She stood firmly behind the desk and shouted at me over and over, kyoki, kyoki, lunacy, lunacy. Where do you sleep around, around, around in the park? The other police were amused and turned away. I stood, and then turned away, but she ordered me to sit back down in the chair.

Who mother?

Okichi.

Your mother?

Okichi.

No, no.

Yes, yes.

No, no, no.

Take my soul.

The police burst into laughter, doubled over, and staggered out of the room. She tried to hold back the derisive laughter, but she could not control the humor over that teaser name. She removed her hat, laughed loudly, and pounded her hands on the desk. Then she recovered and started over.

Who are you?

Ronin Browne.

No, honto ni nai, not truly.

Atomu ainoko.

Yes, ainoko of the ruins.

Where did you buy those socks?

What socks?

The bloated chickens.

My daughter.

Okichi, my mother.

You, you, crazy.

Yes, me, me ronin.

You, police maniac.

The interrogation ended with counterteases. The interpreter boarded the mobile koban. I walked out of the koban on my hands. The police cheered and then drove me back to the river, the scene of the crime. They opened the car door for me, bowed slightly, and waved me out. I heard them say, Police maniac, police maniac. They laughed, bowed, and drove away.

Oshima and several roamers waited for me in the ruins. We cooked rice and vegetables and told stories about the police. The mongrels, feral cats, and other creatures of the ruins were there in time to eat. Tofu, a calico cat, and Tosuto, a wirehaired, crispy mongrel, were always together at the park, the only wild tofu eaters in the ruins. Tosuto, shied by the envy of the other roamer mongrels, was a savage over a photograph of Hirohito.

Why the emperor?

Poetic justice.

By photographs?

Savaged in the ruins.

By a mongrel?

Yes, Tosuto.

Mongrel justice.

Tosuto, for some obscure reason barked, pounced, and stomped the picture of the emperor every time he crossed the circle. Maybe he lost relatives in the war, eaten by soldiers or abused by empire pedigrees. Hirohito was dismembered in the ruins by a ferocious mongrel.

Kitsutsuki once devoured the beaten, photographic remains of the emperor. Hirohito and the militarists aroused the lower pick of officers to abuse their soldiers. The emperor, by his divine, remote manner, deserted the hibakusha of Hiroshima. The empire was a wicked curse that haunted my mother.

Samurai traditions were obscure, the old masters were muted, and the emperor incited the cruelties of the war in his name. Rightly, you see, the emperor on his white horse is always underfoot in the ruins of the Atomic Bomb Dome.

Later that night we created another tricky kabuki version of Rashomon. Kitsutsuki hobbled out of the rain and told horrific war stories. He raised a shadow weapon, fired seventeen times, and counted the prisoners, nurses, and soldiers dead. Crack, crack on his wooden leg, and bodies moldered in his memories of war.

Banka Island.
Listen, crack, crack, crack.
Dead on the beach.
Nurses bear the cross.
Soldiers by number.
Dead again at the gate.

Oshima played the part of a leper who stole hair from bodies abandoned at the gate. Some of the roamers were distraught by the mastery of his kabuki execution, and no doubt they worried that some leper might snatch their hair one night in the peace park.

Naturally, the roamers understood that any pretence of peace was risky, but they were worried about the tatari, the curse and vengeance of those who were incinerated and those burned raw who rushed into the river. The roamers avoided the ghost parade, but now they were constrained by the nuclear kabuki theater.

I assured the roamers that we were evermore secure in the nuclear ruins, and more so because the police named me a maniac. The police would never believe my confessions, stories, or perfect memories in the ruins.

Manidoo Envoy

Ronin created these stories in Atomu 57. He established an original measure of time in the ruins, an ingenious calendar to count the years since the first simulated nuclear peace, August 6, 1945. The Atomu calendar is based on a standard solar year that starts with the nuclear destruction of Hiroshima.

By "simulated peace" he means the fake, sentimental, passive peace of museums and monuments. Japan, he declares, should build a nuclear arsenal, and he argues that nuclear weapons should be monitored by a supranational soldiery.

The Flame of Peace burns perpetually at the end of the Pond of Peace. The flame is set to burn to the end of nuclear weapons in the world. The Cenotaph for victims of the atomic bomb is at the other end of the memorial, where it seems to float in the pond. Ronin set a fire that rushed between the monuments.

Ronin told me he first met Kenzaburo Oe, the distinguished novelist, at the Peace Memorial Museum. He memorized sections of *Hiroshima Notes* in preparation for the chance encounter in the gift shop. Ronin smiled, waved his hand at the tacky tee shirts on display over the counter, and recited these actual words by the author.

"In Hiroshima, I met people who refused to surrender to the worst despair or to incurable madness. I heard the story of a gentle girl, born after the war, who devoted her life to a youth caught in an irredeemably cruel destiny. And in places where no particular hope for living could be found, I heard the voices of people, sane and steady people, who moved ahead slowly but with genuine resolve."

Ronin praised the author, and, at the same time, derided the slogans on the tee shirts. He posed his ridicule as natural reason, the practice of native storiers. Ronin told me that he pointed out the window toward the Flame of Peace and shouted that the flame is a habit not an honor or protest. The flame is a passive promise of nuclear peace, no more than a sentimental flicker of victimry.

Ronin poured gasoline in the pond at the opposite end of the Flame of Peace. Surprisingly, the perpetual flame did not ignite the gasoline. The traces of the blaze were haunting images of the atomic explosion when shadows of incinerated humans were cast on the stone and concrete in Hiroshima. The police made these associations and bowed in shame to the memory of the thousands of dead at the peace memorial.

The Aioi Bridge near the Atomic Bomb Dome was the actual target site. The bridge was repaired after the explosion and used until a new one was constructed in Atomu 38.

Ronin celebrates the roamers as storiers. They are the actual natives of the peace park, the last *ronin* of a great samurai tradition. The police, who were trained to be sympathetic but not romantic about stories, recounted the roamers as street people, and more and more of them gathered every year in the peace park. The police gently rousted them by day when the peace tourists were about and then avoided them at night.

Ronin and Oshima invited certain roamers to eat with them in the nuclear ruins of the Atomic Bomb Dome. After dinner they created kabuki versions of the "Rashomon" story by Akutagawa. Oshima was a lightning chancer, and his kabuki poses were always better in a thunderstorm.

The *kobans* are police posts in urban areas. There are more than six thousand of them around the country. The police *kobans* are an active part of governance in the community. They are familiar with the commerce, crime, and situations of the residents. The police are formal, sympathetic listeners, day and night always on patrol in the community. The *koban* is a service center. Children even come by for candy.

Osaka, a former catch woman, once solicited men for private striptease shows, but now she serves tea to the police and decorates the *koban* with bright flowers. Obviously, her nickname was a disguise. Ronin was truly touched by her coy smile and gestures. Osaka was always ready to tease and be teased in public.

Ronin was detained for interrogation by a special police interpreter at the *koban*, but he was never arrested. The police have the discretion to interview and release anyone, or remove a suspect for arrest at a police station.

Tonase, the police interpreter, was annoyed by his evasive responses and demanded to know his name. Ronin answered, "The courage and loyalty of a samurai warrior remains hidden, untasted, a savor wasted." His response was paraphrased from the first act of the puppet play *Chushingura*, translated by Donald Keene. The poetic phrase "savor wasted" and the notion of being untasted is quoted by the narrator of the play. "The sweetest food, if left untasted, remains unknown, its savor wasted" is from the Chinese. "The same holds true of a country at peace: the loyalty and courage of its fine soldiers remain hidden, but the stars, though invisible by day, at night reveal themselves, scattered over the firmament. Here we shall describe such an instance, a chronicle told in simple language of an age when the land was at peace."

Ronin probably read *Chushingura* when he stayed with me at the Hotel Manidoo. He borrowed many books from my library at the time, including studies of religion and the samurai tradition, and marked two stories, "The Kappa," and "Shiro, The Dog," in *Exotic Japanese Stories* by Akutagawa.

I watched him one morning as he leaned back in his father's chair at the window and browsed through a stack of my books at his side. He lightly touched each paragraph with his fingers until he found an idea or scene of interest, a creative, untested, and liberated reader with a rightful memory.

Ronin mentioned the showy socks the interpreter wore at the *koban*. Several weeks later a newspaper published a story about the roamers, a kabuki leper, and an *ainoko* peace buster. The reporter, a sympathetic young man, caught the interpreter on duty in her wild chicken socks and included that picture in the feature story.

The police wear blue uniforms, and every stitch and fold is regulated, but there is no policy on socks. Singularity is measured by the socks. "Only socks have escaped standardization, and when policemen cross their legs a wide assortment of lengths and colors are displayed," wrote David Bayley in *Forces of Order*.

Faubion Bowers told Ronin that his mother might have been Ainu from Hokkaido. Nightbreaker was the source of that elusive notice, but there is no evidence, not even a name. Ronin, of course, has always been eager to bear that association in memory of his father.

The Ainu are the indigenous natives of the islands of northern Japan. Nightbreaker first learned about the Ainu in a narrative by Ranald MacDonald, a native who taught English in Japan before the arrival of the naval officer and diplomat Commodore Matthew Perry in 1854. The Ainu and the *anishinaabe* told similar stories about natural reason, their creation, animal totems, and survivance.

"Ainu culture is based upon a world view which presumes that everything in nature, be it tree, plant, animal, bird, stone, wind, or mountain, has a life of its own and can interact with humanity," noted Yoshio Sugimoto in *An Introduction to Japanese Society*.

Ronin actually carried out the vision of his father and traveled the same course as Ranald MacDonald. The Ainu would unwittingly engender a presence of his father. Ronin, by his father's unrealized journey, created a union of perfect memories with a native teacher and the Ainu.

Ainu Moshiri is their homeland, a new nation, and a sense of native presence. Nightbreaker might have been part of those stories of revival and survivance at the time, but, in a sense, he was wise to leave that to chance, the miseries of war, and the visionary journey of an unrealized son.

Kitsutsuki is a nickname that means "woodpecker" in Japanese. He earned that obvious name for his many carved and decorated wooden legs. His war stories and death count in the kabuki version of *Rashomon* are similar to the stories told by soldiers and nurses who survived a massacre on Banka Island near Sumatra.

Kitsutsuki was a lieutenant in the same division stationed on the island, but he was never indicted as a war criminal. Ronin learned that he was aware of many details of the massacre, but there were few survivors and no direct evidence that Kitsutsuki was involved in any atrocity.

"At the time of the massacre all nurses were in the uniform of the Australian Military Nursing Service and wearing Red Cross armbands," Yuki Tanaka wrote in *Hidden Horrors*. The nurses reached Radjik Beach on Banka Island and "raised the Red Cross flag, thus clearly indicating they were noncombatants."

Vivian Bullwinkel was the only nurse to survive the massacre on the island. Japanese soldiers shot nurses and bayoneted other prisoners of war, according to war crimes investigations. "All my colleagues had been swept away and there were no Japs on the beach. There was nothing. Just me. I got up, crossed the beach and went into the jungle," wrote Bullwinkel.

Ronin was not aware that the wounded lieutenant had been a suspected war criminal. Kitsutsuki could have been present when the nurses and soldiers, unarmed prisoners, were assassinated at Banka Island.

Hirohito was never honored in the ruins of the Atomic Bomb Dome. Ronin heard stories about the persecution of the *kakure*, or "hidden Christians," when he lived at the Elizabeth Saunders Home. He convinced me that his practice of stomping on pictures of the mighty emperor was an original, specific resistance to the consecration of dominance.

Miki Sawada was moved by the many stories of the *kakure* who were ordered to walk over pictures of Mary and Jesus. The "trampling ceremonies" started in nineteenth-century Japan. Each person was "forced to stomp on a picture of Jesus or Mary as a sign of contempt and renunciation," wrote Elizabeth Anne Hemphill in *The Least of These*. "Some converts waited until the picture was dirty and obscured, and performed the ceremony with a clear conscience."

Ronin pointed out that the police would never believe his stories, and by that strategy of tease and irony he could attack peace fakery with impunity. Remarkably, he reported his acts and thoughts in the dialogue book in the Peace Memorial Museum. Ronin declared that tourists seldom, if ever, take peace messages seriously.

Yesterday, for instance, he wrote in the dialogue book about the actual fire he set on the Pond of Peace. There, in his own cursive words, he reported his actions against the simulations of peace.

Ronin's confession was written under this plaintive note, one of hundreds in the dialogue book: "My name is Anna and I am visiting from U.S.A. I am Japanese but was born in the U.S.A. After the exhibit, I feel very angry and ashamed at my own country. I pray for the world to come to peace. I also pray for this occurrence to never ever happen again anywhere in the world."

DESIGNS OF THE NIGHT SKY

DIANE GLANCY

Encampment

The Dust Bowl (1)

Before

7th April, 1838

The Dream (1)

Jesus

Lifted

The Nests of Boats

A New Sacred Ground

The Stars as Roller Rinks

Whaling

Arrival

The Parents' House

The Librarian

More of the Old Days of Removal

Encampment

Outside the library, the leaves are falling. I think they sound like pages turning as I walk through them. It is sound that carries the story, not the particular words. No. It *was* sound that carried the story.

Inside the library, a young man climbs the stairs to Manuscripts and Rare Books. He is looking for a master's thesis on Cherokee ceremony.

Young Man: "I wanted to know if I was doing the stomp dance the way it'd been done. I asked an elder, he said, oh, it's written down in that library over there."

I take the young man to the theses section.

Are the books content in their encampment in the library? They are cataloged and in their place, yet they circulate. I like to think of them as camps lined up on the hills. One camp can hear others on the shelves. But why are they murmuring, more now than before?

I think of my brothers and their families in their disrupted lives. But Cherokee history is turbulent. There's always been rumblings and uprisings and disagreements. When I open the *Cherokee Observer*, I'm afraid I'll see my brothers' names. Robert Nonoter arrested after a fistfight at the Dust Bowl over tribal politics. Wayne Nonoter arrested, assaulting his wife. Raymond is the only one who usually escapes notice. But he is full of his own hostilities, griefs, and angers. He just doesn't release them. It probably has been two years since he was arrested for brawling.

But Robert is taking up the slack. His children following. Who knows how far they will go?

I'm preoccupied as I walk through the leaves to the house where my daughters, Noel and Nolie, are cooking supper. Wes Stand, Noel's boyfriend, sits with Wayne's children as they watch television. My husband is in his chair reading the newspaper. I sit on his lap, crumpling the paper beneath me. I would stay longer, but Nolie calls me from the kitchen.

Nolie: "Uncle Wayne left Clare, Stu, and Grace and told us not to tell Aunt Cora where they were."

Ada: "She'll know where they are. Where else do they leave their children? Has Cora called?"

Nolie: "No."

Ada: "Where're the girls?"

Noel: "In our room."

Ada: "Your old dolls don't get a rest."

Nolie: "Clare and Grace just like to be in our room."

I think of Wayne with Cora, his wife, after him. At least they'll have a night to fight without the children hearing them.

At least my mother won't call saying the spirits that guard the children are keeping her awake.

But more than Wayne, it's Robert. My oldest brother, Robert.

The Dust Bowl (1)

At the Dust Bowl, Tahlequah's roller rink, my skates are the wheels of a plane. I feel them under me. Where do I go when I take off? The wooded hills and rolling land of northeastern Oklahoma. The post oaks and blackjacks, the corner posts in fields. When I skate at the rink, I am the written word let loose in spoken story. I hear the other voices with which mine can be known. Other voices by which mine will not be alone.

I've known Ether, my husband, since grade school. Our mailbox says *Charles John Ronner*, but he's been called Ether since high school when he put himself to sleep in physics. Ether Ronner is the dirt field from which I take off in my crop duster.

The Dust Bowl was where the wind pulled up tree roots, fence posts, the land itself blew north. I still feel the updraft, uplift, updrift of the wind in my ears. I skate in a whirlwind. Ether is the strength of dust. He is the substance of the land. But I have to have air. The space above the fields of the library where I work.

Ether limits me to four hours at the roller rink on Saturdays. I put on my skates and leave him behind. He never could keep up. All he can do is float through the dust cloud I leave as I take off. Sometimes I hold out my arms. Ada Ronner. I cover ground. Under my rolling feet. My first roller skates were metal frames with wheels I strapped to my shoes. I skated awkwardly over the uneven walks where an old tree had lifted a slab of the walk and I had to jump or else trip. I had walk-skated more than skated, not really rolling anywhere.

My story is the eight small wheels under my feet in the roller rink. A circle within a square, though the building is more of a rectangle, and the rink more of an oval. The roller rink is a trickster hiding its magic, its floor of maple strips, waxed, polished, waiting. I hear the sound of wheels on the floor as I lace the skates on my feet. I hear the old Cherokee voices as I skate. They're from the library also. Maybe Manuscripts and Rare Books is a skating rink for the spirit world. I know the voices talk while they skate. I know I skate with the ancestors. Once they get going.

I look for Robert, my brother, as I skate. He's a truck driver. He can't stop the momentum when he gets back from a long haul. He can't come in off the road. The highway goes on, pulling his truck along with it. He can't sleep, can't sit still in his house. His wife and children are afraid because he looks for a fight to release his tension. I bring him to the rink. Slow him down on skates.

Ada: "When I skate, I feel like you do when you drive."

Robert: "You don't come close."

Ada: "There's a release."

Robert: "You go in circles."

Ada: "Do you remember how we sat on the roof of the pig pen on Grandpa's farm?"

Robert: "I remember Grandpa after me with his switch."

Ada: "The sow would have hurt you."

Robert: "He could have told me to stay out."

Ada: "I think he did. I remembered to stay out of the pen."

Robert: "Too bad we all can't be like you."

Ada: "Feel the wind as you skate, Robert. It's like turning into heaven."

Robert: "Not anywhere near. Heaven is out on the road when you're high on driving and your dreams stomp dance in your head."

Ada: "Why don't you pull off and sleep?"

Robert: (he wants to leave) "I got a timeline to meet."

Ada: "Just keep skating."

Robert: "You're offering me a rink when I need a Roller Derby. A toy truck when I'm used to eighteen wheels."

Ada: "What do you dream, Robert?"

Robert: "The road keeps going and never stops."

Before

Sometimes the voices talk about the old march. From 1820 to 1840, there were several overland trails from the Southeast to Indian Territory, which later became Oklahoma. There were several marches over several years on those trails. But there also had been removal by river. From the Hiwassee in North Carolina, to the Tennessee River, to the Ohio, to the Mississippi, to the Arkansas. *Oars,* I think when I hear the voices. Rowing over river routes at various times in various groups. Flatboats and steamboats without oars.

Maybe Robert is still bound up in the old travel of the tribe. A spirit stuck to him, steaming in the night air. Sometimes I think I feel that spirit. Maybe from the Removal trail. I'm sure I've seen steam rise from Robert when he steps from his rig.

7th April, 1838

The Boats got under weigh this morning at eight and continued to run without any occurrence of importance until near sunset, when we reached Paducah at the mouth of Tennessee River, and anchored a short time near the Town, not willing to land on account of the Indians having access to the Whiskey shops. On attempting to set out again about dark, some water washed into the Keel, (owing to the waves in the Ohio) and the Indians were seized with fear——rushed out of it into the steamboat.

There was no danger, but I found it would be impossible to *convenice* them of that and therefore determined to proceed without the Keel, the S. Boat being large enough to transport the party by giving them the main cabin and lower and forward decks, and having cooking hearths constructed on them later.

The Party having been removed to the S. Boat, we set out from the mouth of Tennessee River about 10 p.m. and are now progressing rapidly toward the mouth of the Ohio.

The Dream (1)

I hear them all. Could imagine them if I didn't. The spirits. The Little People. Over there. On the ridge. They come after dark. I hear them revving their motors on the hill. Their old cars. Fords and Chevys of the spirits. I hear them in the updraft of pines. I see Robert in his rig. The long line of trucks on a vertical road from the earth. The stars as headlights. The spirit warriors with beaded eyes riding on the hood. Trucks ascending and descending on Jacob's ladder (Genesis 28:12). The whole road trembles as if a small helicopter lands with those silent wings that turn on its head. Later the spirits get out their tambourines. They sing their songs to the Maker. The ordinator of the universe. Orator of the world that is both seen and unseen.

Their voices come from dreams.

Who are we to speak?

What have we got to say when there are no answers?

How do we pry the sun out of the ground when it comes up anyway in another place than where we ask?

What do we do in the shadow world?

How do we come back from the edge of the earth?

One spirit is back from an ancient gathering on the northern plains. There's a green spirit with antlers on his head. A yellow spirit who trembles like a stalk of corn. They are a ghostly tribe staying up too late, remembering the Removal trail, the lost years that followed, the boarding school, all weighted with despair.

I hear thunder in my dream. There is lightning from the edge of the hill that is a crooked streak backfiring from Albert Antelope's car.

Why am I a receiver of the voices? A receptor? I might as well stand in an open field with metal curlers during a storm.

Sometimes I dream of the Baptist Church on Sunday. I live in a world neither Jesus, nor the spirits, nor the Little People can fill, but they overlap in places.

I don't like the hymns that tell my voice what to do. I can't read the notes anyway. But when we praise the Maker in church, my voice goes where it wants.

Jesus

We go to church on Sunday. Noel and Nolie are downstairs for their Sunday school class, then they join us for church. Sometimes they sit with their friends.

Jesus, I have given you what you are wishing to get—nails driven by a hammer. And now you have them. Hold them with your strong hands and feet and do not let them go. Jesus, look at us and you will see us come to see you. We will say to one another: "What a great Savior he is! What a holy Savior!" And you, Jesus, will be proud of all that you will hear us say of your greatness. Jesus, do not turn to the sky, but hug the land, for we will cover your body with bluebill duck feathers and the down of an eagle, the chief of all birds; for this is what you are wishing, and this is what you are trying to find from one end of the world to the other.

Lifted

The flock of birds lifts from the field as I pass. Stu watches them as I drive him back to Wayne's. The girls, Clare and Grace, decided to stay with my girls. The birds sound like rustling silk. Mary Nonoter, my mother, feeds the birds. She says she has visions of Indian people in the afterlife, speckled as starlings with spots of light. A whole flock. Across the hills, the gray clouds hang like the net of them flying. The birds could be holes. The spaces between the birds are air. The birds rise as words from one field landing in another. Maybe they are on their way south.

See the horse with mud clomped on his hoofs? His hair matted with rain. Sometimes it rains in clumps. The days are gray for nearly a week. A hurricane on its way north, blowing out as it goes.

There is the land and the sky. Hills and trees. Fields scattered with houses and a barn now and then. A road through them. Somewhere, the Arkansas River that brought some of the ancestors on boats from the original territory in the Southeast. Not the ones that walked, but those who *rowed* the boats.

The spoken words are eating the corn, cooking potatoes. I hear one of the voices telling a story as I drive:

Sound thought it existed all alone. Sound spoke the sky and the land into being because it could shape. If sound kept on with its sound, it always would be all that is. But something else began to be made. Because sound had space, could shape it, could also have shape. Sound made itself into words that could be seen. Words became themselves with themselves. They became rain on the barn. They became the stock in the barn. They became something with shape that could be seen. What is the library but a barn? What are written words but the voice tamed? Domesticated. The written words are animals in their pastures. Fenced. It has to be. Sound has a different way to be recognized. The voice still will be there. It isn't going away. The voice always will be the voice, but now it has another way to say. Sound can be written words. A flock or herd of them. The written words come in books. Shelves hold them. The library is a reminder the written words are stuck in this world. They will not go to the other world the voice alone can transcend.

The Nests of Boats

Manuscripts and Rare Books is in an upstairs corner of the university library. There's an anteroom with the card catalog and librarian's desk, a few cases of Cherokee artifacts, and the cabinet of map drawers. A mural of Cherokee history on the wall. Then there's the large room with a row of windows up near the ceiling. And the shelves of books.

A wire enclosure something like a chicken coop is in a corner of Manuscripts and Rare Books where old books in boxes, genealogies and archives, Cherokee testaments, Cherokee primers, books of magic and old spells, and other rare books, such as *Poor Sarah* and *Relocation*, are shelved.

What should I ask the voices? Why do I hear their murmurings more often now?

In the afternoon, the sky brings in its wet sacks. It is cold and damp. The heat has not been turned on yet. What I want is climate control for the Cherokee books and documents. The ceiling is high. I keep fans running in the corners to circulate air. Once in a while, an official from the Oklahoma Historical Society comes and listens, but nothing is ever done. No thermostat for Manuscripts and Rare Books. In winter, when the heat is on, it rises from the floor below. By May I want to claw out the windows.

It's when I feel the Removal trail by river. Up the Tennessee, the Ohio, the Mississippi, the Arkansas. The nests of boats floating there. The sun coming in as if a window above them.

Someone leaves a *New York Times* on a bench in the anteroom. I see a caption: *Egypt Carvings Set Earlier Date for Alphabet* (John Noble Wilford, Sunday, November 14, 1999). I sit down and read the article:

On the track of an ancient road in the desert west of the Nile—some inscriptions on limestone—earliest known examples of alphabetic writing. The Semitic script with Egyptian influences—dated to somewhere between 1900–1800 B.C.*, two to three centuries earlier than previously recognized uses of a nascent alphabet.*

The alphabet—an invention by workaday people—democratized writing. Alphabetic writing emerged as a shorthand by which fewer than 30 symbols, each one representing a single sound, could be combined to form words for a wide variety of things—and ideas.

The written word left a record. It happened to the Cherokees in 1821 when Sequoyah invented the syllabary. It made an illiterate people literate.

But they still did not write about the Removal trail. That record was left by white lieutenants.

But if it were not for the written word, there would be only a few, floating voices.

Otherwise the journey would be lost.

A New Sacred Ground

When I skate, I can stand on the ridge south of Tahlequah and see the valleys below. What is beyond them? Do I have an atlas? Do I know the old sacred grounds? Where have I gone other than the migrations around the Dust Bowl? Why would I want anywhere else to go? I have a large family:

Rabah, my sister-in-law, married to my oldest brother, Robert, who stews in the heat of the highway, calls: Could I watch their children, Riley and George?

Cora, my sister-in-law, married to Wayne, my middle brother, who doesn't always come home at night, calls: Could I watch their children, Grace, Clare, and Stu?

Shuba, my sister-in-law, married to Raymond, my youngest brother, who is what ______ I hear? (Campaigning for a witch?) Shuba asks: Could I take care of the three boys? Noah, Tubal, and Caleb?

All of them like *tar babies* I can't get my hands back from.

The voices tell stories in the roller rink. *Family is your most important possession*. (Or do I think it's words?)

Ether: "But you don't get anywhere in the roller rink."

Ada: "That's what Robert said. But you travel to the point of departure."

Ether: "Again and again?"

It's written in the sound of my skates. It's the sound of the voice that is the topsoil, lifted up and blown away, turning the sky black with words from their pages.

The Stars as Roller Rinks

While Ether was putting himself to sleep in high school, I wrote a report on roller skating.

Wheeled skates were used in Holland in the eighteenth century, but it was the invention of the four-wheeled skate by J. L. Plimpton in New York in 1863.

Later, the Raymond skate with ball and cone bearing.

The first wheels were made of boxwood, but the wearing of their edges.

Because the ice melted and they wanted to keep going.

I make a creation story. One night, a small comet fell to the earth, leaving a round rink in the ground. Because the stars, the planets, the moons, with their roller skates on. Is why they move around the rink of the sky. I skate with the planets in their orbits around the blackgreen air of the universe.

I name the wheels of my skates.

East. South. West. North.

East. North. West. South.

The Vikings skated on cow ribs or the bones of horses or reindeer, bound to the feet with thongs.

The earliest dated skate was found in Björkö, Sweden, between the eighth and tenth centuries. Bone skates also were found in Norway, Denmark, the Netherlands, England, Germany, Switzerland. I imagine the idea carried on boats across the Atlantic.

The Dutch word, *schaats,* dated from 1573. The word was found in Hexham's 1648 *Dictionarie.*

There was a Scandinavian saga, *Fornmanna Sogur,* 1320.

Samuel Pepys in his 1 December 1662 entry, "people sliding with the Skeats."

John Evelyn in his entry of the same date told of the sliders on the new canal in St. James's Parke. "How swiftly they pass, how suddenly they stop."

I move on the rink in the Dust Bowl. In the old days I could (skate the patterns) *ball of twine, rail fence, straight and curved cut Maltese crosses, hook star, pig's ear star, heel pivot star, Tahlequah grapevine*. While my brothers jumped the ramp of the uneven sidewalk with their bicycles. While they skidded over the gravel roads in their trucks.

The rink is full of Ether's physics. I can feel the four forces as I skate. Gravity. Electromagnetism. The stronger and weaker forces. Ether out of bounds at my discontinuous leaps. My quantum skating.

Whaling

Whale, I have given you what you are wishing to get—my good harpoon. And now you have it. Hold it with your strong hands and do not let go. Whale, turn toward the beach and you will see the young men come down from my village to see you; and the young men will say to one another: "What a great whale he is! What a fat whale he is!" And you, whale, will be proud of all that you will hear them say. Do not turn outward, but hug the shore, for when you come ashore, young men will cover your great body with bluebill duck feathers and with the down of the great eagle, the chief of all birds; for this is what you are wishing, and this is what you are trying to find from one end of the world to the other.

Arrival

I became a Christian because they teach forgiveness.
In the old Indian way, no one forgave anything.
—Agnes Pumpkin

I walk up the hill from school. Before I turn the corner onto Summit, I hear Raymond's boys, Noah, Tubal, and Caleb (I want to call him Cain) yelling in the yard. Wes's art car covered with fishing lures and a small outboard motor is parked at the curb. Where are Noel and Nolie, my girls? They're supposed to be watching their cousins.

I never know where the boys are headed or what's going to be left after they've gone. Tubal is chasing Noah with a stick as long as he is. They have torn down some of the woodpile crawling over it. The neighbor's dog is barking. I call to the boys (my nephews) to stop fighting. They run past me through the yard.

Ada: "Where's your father? That tribal election can't be over soon enough. Where's Shuba? Conjuring her spells? Why am I the dumping ground for everyone's children?"

Inside, Nolie is in the kitchen making Rainy Mountain with her mashed potatoes. Wes and Ether have their feet on the low table in front of the sofa.

Ada: "Get those boys in here. Tie them to their chairs at the table."

Ether: "I'll bring 'em in."

Wes: "I can't stay."

Nolie: "Eey yaw, Dad, go get 'em."

Wes drives off, the propeller on his outboard turning.

Ether ropes the boys in their chairs.

Nolie: "Grandma called. She wants you to take her to the doctor."

Ada: "Has she forgotten I work? Has she forgotten what it's like to have children scattered all over the house?"

Noel: "Wes and I will take her after school."

Ada: "I've got to go to the grocery too—for the cookout over there. My sisters-in-law could do some of the shopping."

The Parents' House

We go to our parents' house.

THE PARENTS: Obed and Mary Nonoter.

The three brothers and their families:

Robert and Rabah, their children, Riley and George.

Wayne and Cora, Stu and the girls, Clare and Grace.

Raymond and Shuba, the boys, Noah, Tubal, and Caleb.

Sometimes the Stands, so they can see their son, Wes, as they say.

Sometimes Ether's parents. His sister.

Sometimes neighbors we've known since we were children.

Sometimes friends of the children.

Then, of course, Ether (Charles John Ronner) and Ada (me), our daughters, Noel and Nolie. (Noel is the reason Wes Stand is always at our house.)

We gather in my parents' backyard to cook. It's still warm. Sometimes the children, hot and sweaty after running in the yard, take off their sweaters. Then Rabah, Cora, and Shuba yell at the children to put their sweaters back on before they chill. My girls, Noel and Nolie, run after the children to corral them again.

Robert, Wayne, and Raymond huddle as if boys wanting to retreat into the backseat of the family car, as if remembering when they made their own way down the road without families and responsibility; when they were the responsibility our parents had. They are grouchy with their wives and children; they are at odds with the world in which they have to live, unable to catch up with whatever moves ahead of them, always behind, overwhelmed at every turn. They are angry and hurt; they flee to the wildlife refuge of their arguments. They claw at one another and play out their wars on themselves.

Maybe they are afraid of being husbands and fathers because it is a difficult instinct. It splays them between self and offspring. Which would survive? Could both? Maybe they didn't have enough of themselves to disperse to anyone. Why? Maybe it was growing up Cherokee in Cherokee County.

Ether turns the burgers. Why is he different from my brothers? What happened that made him want to have ideas in his head like constellations? Why are others left out? Robert thinking of the load he pulls in his truck; Wayne his construction work; Raymond, what job does he have now?

I hear the voices of Robert and Wayne. Robert has him in the ditch by the creek behind my parents' house. Cora yelling that Robert will break Wayne's neck.

Their voices are a tag team of crows in the trees, or starlings at dusk, or the locusts that come in seven-year plagues to deafen the evening with their noise. How they argue. Wild and helpless.

My father is there now, pulling apart two of his sons. Wes's father, Wes, and Ether are there; the neighbors coming now. I don't know where Raymond is. Robert must have had a few beers before he came. There's no drinking on my father's property. None. If they want to drink, they have to do it before they come.

The children are crying in fear of the men's violence, or they are fighting among themselves. Stu is the only one too young to understand, but this time even he seems to look with recognition.

But what is there to understand? The Cherokees are roily as if they just stepped off the boats after Removal, ready to kill those who signed the treaty. What has changed?

Shuba comforts my mother, who is crying.

My father pulls Robert and Wayne to the yard. He sits them in the lawn chairs and stands beside them. I see the veins stand out in his neck. How many times have my brothers wrecked our cookout? How many times have we eaten with anger stuffed in our throats?

Ada: "What if the children act like you?"

Robert: "You're the only one with a cowbell around your neck."

I'm not sure what he means, but Ether seems angry. I remind him of the burgers (charred) and he takes them off the grill.

My mother calls everyone to the table. Robert and Wayne stand up, their legs unstable as if they just got off the boat.

The Librarian

I didn't want to be a librarian. I didn't know what else I wanted to do. Ether knew from the beginning he wanted to study physics. His mother hung stars over his crib; he reached for them since he was an infant. When Ether went to the University of Oklahoma for his Ph.D. in physics, I studied at Northeastern State University in Tahlequah and worked in the library and skated at the rink. Ether returned to Northeastern to teach because I didn't want to leave Tahlequah.

I kept working at the library, kept taking courses. Maybe the library is my city of refuge. (Among the cities, six shall be for a refuge (Christ) which you shall assign for the manslayer that he might flee there (Numbers 35:6).)

But if I was going to be a librarian, I didn't want to work in Manuscripts and Rare Books. I wanted to be in Acquisitions or Circulation or Reference or Periodicals, where I could be on the floor. Where I could see others. But I was put on the second floor in the archives where a student comes in and I have to make sure the book is handled properly, not permitted to leave the reading room, nor marked in. I assist those who do research and want the old voices. The stories of the Cherokee tribe were recorded by soldiers during the Removal, by ethnographers, by the WPA project. Some of the books are chants and old magic. Before they knew stories weren't to be written. Or early writers or early writings of other writers. Or early editions or whatever came under the heading of Manuscripts and Rare Books. Whatever could be gathered in Special Collections.

I begin to think the books want me here. They want me to hear what they say. They talk from the written word. Maybe writing doesn't kill the voice. Put it in a grave. Maybe writing isn't the destroyer people think it is.

Sometimes ethnographers wrote down the voices in their own way. The ethnographers didn't always get it right. Or if they did, the voices didn't want to be written. They try to get out of the writing as if it were a straight jacket or restraining order. Sometimes I know the murmurings I hear are the voices struggling to cover themselves; to get out of the books. But where would they go?

More of the Old Days of Removal

I sit in Manuscripts and Rare Books. No one comes to ask for assistance. I open the papers of the Cherokee Emigration. I feel the oars in my hand.

9th April, 1838

We reached Memphis last night about 12 p.m. and stopped a short time to procure some Fresh Beef and other supplies. The Boat then continued to run (stopping once to wood) until about 3 o'clock this afternoon, when we reached Montgomery's Point and there stopped in the stream a short time to take in a Pilot for the Arkansas River. We then entered White River, passed thro' the cut-off, and are now ascending the Arkansas and are about 50 miles above *it's* mouth (9 o'clock p.m.). We find the Arkansas not very high, but shall probably be able to reach Little Rock and may perhaps go higher. The present party has been subsisting since starting on Bacon, Pork, Flour meal, and a small quantity of Fresh Beef.

10th April, 1838

We continued to run last night until about 11 o'clock when a slight accident happened to the machinery, the Boat was obliged to lie by 3 or 4 hours, and then set out again and continued to run (stopping once to wood) from that time until this evening about 7, and then stopped for the night, it being too dark, and the water too shallow to proceed until the morning. We are now 40 or 50 miles below Little Rock.

11th April, 1838

The Boat got under weigh this morning early and reached Lt. Rock about ½ past 11 a.m. I had her anchored in the stream to prevent access to Whiskey and went on shore for the purpose of consulting the Principal Disbursing Agent as to the probability of being able to proceed further up the river on *The Smelter.*

I found it would be useless to attempt to proceed further in a Boat of her size, and therefore made an arrangment with the S. Boat *Little Rock* which is, I found on the point of setting out for the upper Parts with two Keels in tow.

The Captain agreed to take the present Party as far up as possible for $5 each for the whole distance and proportionately for less, which I ascertained to be a reasonable term, and the best arrangement I could possibly make at present. The Party is to have the entire use of one Keel, the Top of the other, & all parts of the S. Boat except the cabins. After landing some provisions from *The Smelter* I proceeded with the Party on board of her, about 5 miles above the town and landed for the night.

I purchased to day under authority from the Superintendent of the Cherokee Emmigration, Eighty Barrels of (cheap?) Pork, and Eighty barrels of Flour, and turned them over to the Principal Mil. Disb. Agent at Little-rock, for the use of the Cherokee Emmigration in the ensuing summer & fall. I obtained this provision by paying only it's cost and carriage.

12th April, 1838

The Little Rock Keels are heavily loaded the other nearly empty and fitted up for the Indians——arrived last night at the point at which I stopped the Party, and early this morning the people and their Baggage were transfered from *The Smelter.* We then immediately got under weigh and proceeded 5 or 6 miles, when the heavy Keel sprung a leak from running on a Bar or Snag, whereupon the Captain found it necessary to run ashore to prevent her from sinking. The whole day has been consumed in getting out the Freight from this Keel and stopping the leak.

I have determined, if possible, to induce the Captain to leave his heavy Keel and all his freight, and take with all possible dispatch, as beside other reasons the Small-Pox is in this section of country, a disease, apparently of all other the most fatal to Indians.

14th April, 1838

The Indians were got on board this morning at light and the boats have continued to run thro' the day, only stopping a short time to Wood, and by 3 o'clock p.m. had come 50 miles and reached White's on Lewiston Bar 4 miles below that place. The Keel was then landed and every means——.

15th April, 1838

This morning after the people had their breakfast, they walked about 5 miles up the south bank of the Arkansas for the purpose of lightening the Boat. A different channel was then tried by the Captain with success, and by noon we reached a second Bar about 2 miles above Lewiston.

16th April, 1838

The forenoon spent in trying to force the S. Boat over the Bar without effect, and the afternoon was consumed in getting her ashore on the north bank of the river.

17th April, 1838

Much rain fell last night and the people not having Tents, I found it necessary to hire a small house to protect them from the weather. This morning another trial was made to go over the Bar which was successful, and about 11 a.m. the S. boat reached the point which the Indians were encamped and after taking the Party on board continued to run until a short time after dark, and stopped for the night at the foot of Five Island, having come between 30 & 40 miles. Rations of Prime *Vork,* Fresh Beef & Flour were issued to day for 4 days as usual.

Edwd. Deas
Liet. U.S. Army
Conductor

Contributors

Stephen Graham Jones is Blackfeet and the author of five novels, *Bleed into Me, The Fast Red Road, The Bird is Gone, All the Beautiful Sinners,* and *Demon Theory.* A visionary storier, Jones has created marvelous, fantastic narratives at the ironic edge of ordinary experience and reality. He is a professor of English at the University of Colorado, Boulder.

Eric Gansworth, an enrolled member of the Onondaga Nation, was born and raised at the Tuscarora Indian Nation in western New York. He is the author of six books, *Indian Summers, Nickel Eclipse: Iroquois Moon, Smoke Dancing, Mending Skins, Breathing the Monster Alive,* and *A Half-Life of Cardio-Pulmonary Function,* and he edited the anthology *Sovereign Bones: New Native American Writing.* Gansworth is a professor of English and the Lowery Writer-in-Residence at Canisius College in Buffalo, New York.

Frances Washburn is Lakota and Anishinaabe and lived on the Pine Ridge Reservation in South Dakota. She is an assistant professor of American Indian studies and English at the University of Arizona at Tucson. *Elsie's Business* is an outstanding, engaging narrative of a native community and survivance.

Gerald Vizenor is Anishinaabe and a member of White Earth Reservation in Minnesota. He is the author or more than twenty books, including *The People Named the Chippewa, Manifest Manners, Fugitive Poses, Dead Voices, Bear Island: The War at Sugar Point,* and *Almost Ashore.* He won the American Book Award for *Griever: An*

American Monkey King in China. Vizenor is a professor of American Studies at the University of New Mexico, Albuquerque, and Professor Emeritus at the University of California, Berkeley.

Diane Glancy is Cherokee and a poet, novelist, and playwright. She is the author of more than thirty books, novels, poetry volumes, and plays, including *Stone Heart: A Novel of Sacajawea, The Cold-and-Hungry Dance, The Mask Maker, Trigger Dance, Primer of the Obsolete, The Shadow's Horse,* and *American Gypsy: Six Native American Plays*. She won the North American Indian Prose Award for *Claiming Breath*. Glancy is a professor of English and creative writing at Macalester College.

In the Native Storiers series:

Mending Skins
by Eric Gansworth

Designs of the Night Sky
by Diane Glancy

Bleed into Me: A Book of Stories
by Stephen Graham Jones

Hiroshima Bugi: Atomu 57
by Gerald Vizenor

Native Storiers: Five Selections
edited and with an introduction
by Gerald Vizenor

Elsie's Business
by Frances Washburn

To order or obtain more information
on these or other University of Nebraska
Press titles, visit www.nebraskapress.unl.edu.